A DAY WITH THE OLD FOLKS

VERDUN, 1916

MICHAEL P. KIHNTOPF

outskirtspress
DENVER, COLORADO

A Day with the Old Folks
Verdun, 1916
All Rights Reserved.
Copyright © 2015 Michael P. Kihntopf
v3.0

Cover Image by Michael P. Kihntopf

Outskirts Press, Inc.
http://www.outskirtspress.com

ISBN: 978-1-4787-5650-7

Library of Congress Control Number: 2015906185

Outskirts Press and the "OP" logo are trademarks belonging to Outskirts Press, Inc.

PRINTED IN THE UNITED STATES OF AMERICA

Chapter 1
0300 - 0600

E scape. The fleeting breeze that caressed the downy cheek of nineteen year old Peter Lange offered an escape in its soft eddies. Lange sat at the roots of an ancient forest that was bare of leaves yet the light wind managed to stir memories of the faint rustling of leaves that had echoed through the branches for countless centuries. A dream took form. Lange's young, agile mind cloaked in darkness by the night and closed eyes, took wing on the breeze transporting him over the surrounding wood. The night's blackness cleared suddenly in a flash to show sunlit cloudless azure skies. He imagined himself soaring in those skies. Billowing clouds rushed by sending out cottony tendrils that tried to snag him as he climbed to loftier heights. Instinctively, he stretched his body into a thin javelin shape to gain speed but, like Icarus, who got too close to the sun, he found himself plunging toward the earth in a head over heals tumble. There were intermittent glimpses of the earth in all its brownness getting closer by the second. His hands went out before him in a vain effort to stop the tumbling, slow his descent but ultimately to break his fall when that should occur. Just before what would appear to be an impact, the tumbling stopped. He had a clear look at the flat earth. He closed his eyes expecting a bone crushing impact, instead the ground parted ahead of his flattened palms as if it was water. For a moment he was plunged back into darkness. A feeling of despair overcame him in a sickening, stomach turning moment. Then the black parted. He no longer saw himself as a fleeting soul free of earthly bounds but as a disgraced medieval knight condemned to a dank, reeking prison beneath his liege lord's keep. What crime he had committed was a mystery but he sensed that his wrong doing had something to do with a betrayal of trust and loyalty. Chained to a crumbling, moldering wall, he surveyed his prison in the dim flickering light that a half meter window allowed in. Everything was either brown or black with age. The stone walls were wet with moisture that dripped to the floor in an almost steady stream. Puddles had formed here and there. The shortness of his fetters forced him to stand in one of those puddles. His boots were soaked through and his toes were numbed by a bitter cold.

A scratching noise distracted him. He leaned his ear in its direction. It was the only sound to be heard besides his own heavy breathing. For a few seconds he held his breath to determine the noise's origin and identify it. Could it be someone coming to release him? Then he realized that the noise came from rats squabbling in the walls probably over tidbits they may have stolen from some neglected plate or from the corpse that he somehow knew resided in the next cell. He was sure that their food had not come from his meal since he had not been given anything to eat or drink for a number of days. Hunger and thirst tormented him as much as the anguish of self pity he felt over his perceived crimes.

As if to rescue him, the light breeze returned and pulled at his chains jingling them ever so softly but the prison's air, as thick as a seaborne fog, attempted to swallow the wind covering it with the smell of spoiled, maggot infested meat tinged with the reek of human excrement and burning sulfur. The wind turned away from the fetid atmosphere soaring above it to tantalize Lange's nostrils with a faint smell of almonds. The faint jingling of his chains became the clamor of a Chinese gong and the scratching in the walls turned to a shout. Lange opened his eyes to his reality.

"Gas!" Lange's feet jerked as if to run causing a small tidal wave in the ankle deep puddle of water that surrounded them. His hands fumbled at the container of his gas mask. In seconds, his face was wrapped in rubberized cloth. For a few minutes he lost sight of the world around him as the mask's lenses fogged over as a result of his now pent up breath. He almost gave way to the darkness to recapture his dream but his self preservation instinct brought him back. He opened his eyes and patiently waited for the fogging on the goggles to evaporate. Soon the glasses cleared and Lange could see that he was perched on the slope of an artillery shell hole that was over three meters wide and a few meters deep. The coat of mail he had worn in his daydream had become the field gray uniform of an infantry soldier. Around him lay the blackened, splintered stumps of an ancient forest that had been the victim of the constant artillery shelling over the last two years. Their once majestic trunks lay about the landscaped like so many discarded, unburied bodies indistinguishable from the human corpses that lay among them in various states of decomposition over which rats raced in a mad game of tag. It was hard to determine if an upright limb was that of a man or a tree. He often asked himself as he looked over the sea of bodies to see one of those sticks extending in an almost perpendicular angle from the ground if it was a man's arm or a tree limb which reached to the sky as if imploring the heavens to give aid and rescue them from the brownish sludge that the once nourishing ground had become. Rains and incessant artillery shell explosions had turned the once rich soil into oozing mire which wrapped desperation over everything.

Lange was one member of an eight man section that occupied a string of unconnected shell holes which comprised a listening station or sap a few meters in front of the main company line. That particular sap was closer to the enemy's positions than to his own lines. Such a position was advantageous as well as dangerous. From there his section could listen and observe. Should the enemy begin to mass for an attack, Lange and his companions could warn the company. The section leader was to shoot up a green flare as a sign of assault then the section would hold their ground offering the first taste of rifle fire to the assailants. The sap was a suicide position. Lange was sure that the enemy knew of its location although there was no indication on their part that his opinion was true. If they did indeed know of its existence, to ensure the success of any assault, grenadiers would be sent in front of the main attack to kill everyone in the sap. All eight of them knew that at any second hand grenades could arc over the craters' lips. The French bombs were not at all as deadly as they were disorientating. Their blasts threw up pea size fragments and any loose debris near the explosion. The blast, smoke, and flying objects made sight and hearing impossible for a few seconds. The death came with the men that followed the detonations armed with all sorts of weapons. Then there would be a hand to hand fight in which his section, because of its low numbers in comparison to a strong attacking force, would either be killed or taken prisoner. Escaping to the company's main line of defense was out of the question since the distance was too far and the French machine guns were too accurate in firing at fleeing soldiers. The foe's machine guns would cut them down after just a few paces. Lange hoped that his end would come quickly. Either hands up or a shot to the head was preferable to an agonizing lingering death that a stab with a bayonet would bring.

After painting that picture, Lange sketched another. He shivered thinking about the alternative to hand to hand combat: artillery barrage. He had heard that quite often the French preferred not to sacrifice an assault team. Instead they would send over a few high explosive shells. High explosive shells tore themselves apart in ferocious bangs that threw huge chunks of metal in all directions. Many of the shards were razor sharp and as big as meat platters. They flew through the air like Olympic discuses severing limbs from bodies in lightning speed or ripping open torsos with the precision of butcher's meat cleavers. He had heard of men who had suffered these types of wounds writhing in pain for hours on end, unattended in no man's land, before they died. Sometimes, a hero crawled out to bring one of these men back but there was no solace in rescue. Such dismembered or gashed men were whisked off to surgeons who thought themselves also to be heroes because they stuffed entrails back into position with minor paring or kept a man without arms or legs alive. In their self inflicted glory they failed to see how helpless such men would become in a society that shunned war cripples. Lange's mind was made up. A hand to hand fight was preferable. He mentally erased the sketch of mutilation caused by artillery.

The landscape was far from silent in those early morning hours. Artillery shells burst above and on the company lines some twenty meters to the rear of Lange's shell hole. That could be a sign that the enemy did not know of the sap's position although the artillery's range could change in the blink of an eye. The barrage that they were currently experiencing had lasted four days. From those explosions had come the warm breeze that had attempted to transport Lange away. The noise was deafening but he had learned to mute the din until it sounded like the noises of a busy street in his hometown of Berlin. But even with this ability to deaden the mind numbing din of detonations, Lange did not lose the ability to distinguish the noise of nearing danger. Nearly eight months of front line duty had trained him to recognize distinctive sounds. The clank of a mess tin or a shout stood out like a sour note in a Bach fugue or like a dog yapping at the horses' hooves on the street. There were many mornings when Lange could plainly hear the song of a meadow lark over the noise of the artillery's roar.

Crouching beside Lange was three of his section mates,

Liebermann, Kowalski, and Kluggmann. They had heard the gas warning and had also donned their masks. Their otherwise human faces had taken on the shapes of frog like monsters with pale skin and bulging eyes and a huge round mouth that looked cavernous. They were almost indistinguishable but Lange had long ago recognized traits and body postures that gave away identities no matter how deep the mud was encrusted on uniform and face or how fantastically gas masks had disguised their faces. He could distinguish his section mate, Liebermann, because of the slimness of his body and his vulture like posture. He squatted on a little lip of the crater's wall looking into the slimy water at the bottom of the shell hole. Like Lange, thirst tormented him. He knew that within Liebermann's skull resided a brain that connived day and night to secure sustenance to eat or drink. Even with the mask on, Lange could see that his mind was thinking out some sort of scheme to get food or water. He was an eating machine, a profession that should not be brought to the army or war. There was no end to what he would do for just one more bite of food or sip of drink than anyone else had. Some even said that he would trade his mother for enough food to satisfy his gargantuan appetite. Lange knew better. Liebermann had never had a mother to trade.

Emil Kowalski, lying on his back next to Liebermann, was the thinker of the section. His favorite position was looking to the heavens for an answer. Although the mask covered Kowalski's face, Lange knew that his eyes were wide open and fixed on some star that he could name. Every platoon had a philosopher like Kowalski or was reputed to have one. A man who had the answer to every question or could reason out a solution that made officers look like village idiots. He was the source of pride to the rest of the platoon and a constant topic of either awe or jokes on just how dumb smart people can be when faced with practical knowledge applications. Kowalski's favorite topic was reasoning out his part in the overall destiny of the world and explaining it to others. He expounded on that subject, of which he had deep personal experiences, in great detail. He would always begin, to those who had not heard his dissertation before, by describing himself as a victim of destiny and the target of those who would have him out of the way because of his great intellect. Some, upon hearing those opening lines, would walk away or roll over and feign sleep. But there were others who were like fish who gapped at the offered bait on the end of a mental hook wondering if there was food or doom to be had. They would sit or stand before Kowalski with open mouths waiting for the bait to get closer mesmerized by the impending death that they approached. To those he would continue his tale.

Kowalski's persecution had started early; as he completed the elementary years of his education where he had formed aspirations of attending university. His teachers had encouraged him to aspire toward such heights through numerous compliments about his intellect to other students. Their words of praise had fed his ego while they had slashed at those who were financially and socially worthy of a university position but not so mentally gifted. However, his hopes had been dashed. Because of his humble birth as the son of a construction laborer, some lothario had denied him access to the vine covered halls and condemned him to toil at the mortar mixing troughs as his father had done. There was no changing of his stars as the teachers had insinuated. All the back breaking mental gymnastics he had performed had been for nothing. He had taken the menial work in stride and kept the fires of aspirations burning. His extra pennies went to buying books, newspapers, pamphlets, any written treatise which he devoured in his free time. Like Voltaire, he felt close to finding out God's purpose by reasoning the Supreme Being's existence when the biggest injustice of his life fell upon him. Conscription.

Kowalski had known that the inevitable day for joining the army was nearing but he chose, as so many thinkers did, to ignore it. Germany had been at war for nearly six months when he was called and it was as if he had slept in a cave during that time. His barrack mates scoffed at him when he confessed that he was unaware of the first battles and did not know who the enemy was or why they were fighting. It was during his initial infantry training that Kowalski had an epiphany. In the middle of bayonet practice his mind seized upon a thought that electrified the rest of his intellect. War was barbarity! It was a return to living under animal instincts instead of reason. Those two statements fostered even greater concepts over the remaining training days and culminated at the shock of hearing the first shots directed at him by an enemy that wanted to kill him. In an instant he saw himself as a natural savage. It was in that state, as Rousseau had said; man would realize the plan of God. As a savage he saw that the war would finally bring about the great revolution which would free those such as him from the tyranny of the class structure. During the dissertation of these revelations to those who would listen, Kowalski's voice would start at a soft tone and gradually rise to a crescendo with the last few words. Then he would sit back as if exhausted to observe the impact of his words upon his listeners. Some faces were blank, others were apprehensive, while the remaining ones were glad that the voice had died and they had an excuse to go on some trivial but important errand.

Then there was Kluggmann, on Lange's right. He lay prone at the shell hole's rim looking out over the surrounding dark terrain like a panther waiting to spring on unsuspecting prey that might be passing by. He was a professional soldier; one of many retired career noncommissioned officers who the government had recalled after the first battles had taken their toll among officers and sergeants of the regular, standing army. Higher headquarters had scattered these encrusted, aged veterans through the depot regiments from which they had already stripped all able bodied leaders. His charge had been to train volunteers and conscripts and accompany them into the field where his professionalism would add backbone to the doubtful courage of the new recruits.

Although Kluggmann had attained the rank of sergeant often in his career, his taste for pleasure had stunted his career. After nineteen years of service he could claim only the rank of gefreiter but he had experience. He had had the distinction of having shot at Chinese, Africans, and an assortment of Europeans in wars in Asia and Africa through his years. That was his distinction. He was a killer. He did not lament his position or the killing. He was not a romantic who found grief in the taking of lives or lay awake nights visualizing the faces of those he had killed. He coldly viewed soldering and all the violence that went with it as his job. In his mind, killing was no different than Lange's position as a gymnasium student.

The group had been together since February 1915; longer than any other section mates. What was very odd was that after nearly one year they were still able to talk to one another without getting into arguments or coming to blows. It seemed that their differences were acceptable to each other no matter how deviant or strange they might be. They laughed at the same jokes seeing the punch line instantly and they understood each other's opinions without having to question the details. Even Kowalski's reasoning chats did not bore them. That was not the case with other sections who became antagonists within weeks after being grouped together. These four were different. Initially, the other members of the company called them the Brothers but that label fell out of favor as men came and went. After a while they were introduced as the Old Folks to those who came to replace the casualties. That name seemed appropriate since none of them had succumbed to capture, death, or wounds as had the rest of the section and the company.

A section was eight riflemen. The Old Folks had weathered through the other four who had augmented their ranks quite often.

Normally, such longevity in combat would garner respect and awe but in the case of these four, people were afraid to be assigned to their section. Rumor had it that the Old Folks sucked all the good luck out of others. No one wanted to be in their presence for too long. Replacements to the second section of the first platoon were dutifully warned about the Old Folks and advised to get out as soon as possible. Unluckily for the majority of the new assignees, none survived long enough to move on to other combat duties unless it involved a stay in hospital.

As Lange looked over his three companions he realized that the other four section members were no where to be seen. Despite the room in that hole, the rest of the section had sought refuge in other craters. Involuntarily he shook his head from side to side neither approving nor disapproving of their fears but finding humor in them. He even questioned why he was there with those people. What would his mother have said about this group he had fallen in with? She would have disapproved, that was for sure. A sneak thief, a killer, and an intellectual. How did he fit into that mess? He was a volunteer from the benches of academia, destined to become a member of the ruling class of bureaucrats. Yet with those three he felt a refreshing release from the beef and potatoes every night for supper world.

An artillery round burst to Lange's right scattering shrapnel bullets in every direction but not into his hole. The four pressed themselves against the shell hole's walls and tried to shrink their whole bodies under their new steel helmets for protection. Another round that burst to the left was followed by screams from the rest of the section who had sheltered in that direction. Lange's soldier instinct told him a third round would land on him and his mates. He decided to find another hole. As Lange rose, so did the others. They had made no signs to one another nor were they able to shout words above the din of bursting rounds; it was as if they thought with the same brain. They crouched low and moved like a cat with eight legs clearing the lip of their crater and running to the place where the last round had landed. A few machine guns' bullets kicked up clots of earth at their heels but it was not aimed fire. The debris created by the explosions and the darkness obscured their movements. Could these shells indicate that their sap had been seen? Shells arced overhead indicating that the explosions may have been short rounds. There was still a chance that the French had not seen their position.

In the new hole, they found two dead and one wounded. Another was buried by the earth that the exploding shell had kicked up. The four knew that digging for him was a waste of time. He had probably suffocated a few minutes after being buried or his limbs would be mangled and he was no use as a fighter. Liebermann bandaged the wounded man as best he could. There were multiple holes to plug. He used the first aid package that the wounded man carried and the ones from the dead men. He retained his packet for himself. Liebermann begrudged the waste of the bandages on others but he had a romantic side in his attitude. He knew that the man would eventually die through neglect since the stretcher bears had all been killed two days ago and none of the rest of the section could afford the time to drag him back to an aid station. Yet he wanted the man to die fulfilled rather than in agony, an agony brought on by a feeling of neglect. A bandaging always gave hope to a hopeless cause. The man would think that there was a chance of survival even though he also knew that there was no one to take him away in time.

Lange looked out over the crater's lip to ascertain his whereabouts and the location of the company strong points. He tried to find the landmarks that he had noted during the move up to the sap. They were gone or, at least, indistinguishable in the darkness and because of the fine, mist like soil that the exploding shells turned into the air. The flash of fire of each detonation also served to blind him as a tray of photographic flash powder would. From behind, he felt a violent tug. Kluggmann had grabbed his coattails and pulled him away from the edge.

"You, keep your head done like I showed you. If anyone is out there", he shouted in his gruff, throaty voice close to Lange's ear, "they will make themselves known as time wears on. Sooner or later they'll want to see how badly we died. They're a gory lot. Let them come to us and see what it gets them. You're safe here." Kluggmann was not only a trainer; he was the shepherd of the bunch.

Albert Kluggmann thought about himself as Lange stared at him. He was a professional soldier who had always had the shepherd instinct. His army career had started because of that trait. It was in another life. When he was sixteen. He and a few mates had been drinking heavily after fourteen hours in the coal mine. They had decided to get stinking drunk. Their reasoning was that since the following day was the Sabbath and therefore a day off having a hangover would not be a liability. They could sleep it off and be steady on their feet when Monday came around along with the dangers of pick mining. As long as their money lasted the beer flowed. Toward early morning they had all decided that they were hungry. The barmaid and cook had long since departed so there was no food to be had on the premises. They had risen from their glasses in a feigned attitude of annoyance railing on the sad state of service in an otherwise prestigious establishment and staggered from the beer garden to the grocers a few houses away to buy something to eat. But the shop had been closed. They had banged on the door and shouted for the grocer to wake up and open the store. They shouted that they were hard working miners who fed the industry of Germany with sweat drenched coal and deserved to be honored. Stray dogs barking at the top of their lungs accompanied the miners hollering. Finally, after what felt like hours, the owner had stuck his head out of his second floor apartment window and told them to go away or he would call for the police. The youths had refused to leave and took to banging harder and screaming more loudly, if that were possible, for the grocer to open. Their redoubled efforts were rewarded by the contents of the chamber pot. Outraged they tore open the door and began helping themselves to whatever came to hand. A light flashed and the store owner thundered down the back stairs that connected his shop and apartment. Kluggmann grabbed his compatriots by their collars and threw them out into the street where they scattered in all directions suddenly very sober. The grocer was shouting for the police as Kluggmann made sure all his friends were out. To slow the owner he picked up a can of peaches and threw it at him as he turned to run into the street to save himself. There was a scream and he heard the man shout 'Kluggmann, you'll pay.' The grocer had recognized him as a regular visitor of his daughter.

When the police came to the mine on Monday to arrest Kluggmann he found out that the randomly thrown can had hit the grocer fully in the face and the poor man was teetering on the edge of death. Kluggmann had stood before the magistrate who asked for the names of his accomplices. Kluggmann remained silent. The police beat him, but Kluggmann remained silent. Two days later, after the grocer's medical state had progressed toward recovery, the same judge gave Kluggmann a choice of ten years in prison or twelve years with the Kaiser's army. Kluggmann chose the latter hoping that he would be able to desert once he was released to the army's care. He was not allowed such a chance. A sergeant was in the courtroom. In chains, he was hustled off to Bremen and thrown into the brig of a ship. Four months later he disembarked in the new colony of German Southwest Africa where he became an enforcer of a German peace among the native populations.

After a rudimentary training, Kluggmann chased dissidents to German rule across savannah and desert with the orders to shoot first and capture second. His native opponents were armed with spears of which they were very deadly if involved in close combat.

But Kluggmann carried a Mauser rifle capable of killing at three hundred meters and he learned to use this advantage with remarkable ease. Many unsuspecting native prey fell dead before they heard the report of his rifle. He even learned to use a bayoneted rifle with deadly agility. When ambushed by his foe, he parried and slashed with the best of them finally bringing them down with one thrust or a swift slash across the neck or belly. Each combat triumph was an eroding factor toward the idea of desertion. Eventually he accepted his lot.

The army became his way of life. It provided him with food, clothing, shelter and pay. His duty was in the wild outdoors. He wanted for nothing. He often reasoned with himself that had he not thrown that fate filled can, chances were that he would have died in the mines a stunted broken man. In Africa, he grew stout and even more muscular. His face took on a healthy tan and he commanded respect even among the wealthiest when he swaggered along the garrison town's dusty streets. His officers soon forgave him for his previous way of life and noted how efficient he was as a soldier. But beneath the ardor of his new career an addiction took hold and grew.

The thrill of the chase and kill was accompanied by a surge in adrenalin. The natural stimulus coursed through his veins at every encounter giving him the feelings of a primal beast. It took away pain and heightened his awareness. Patrols became hunting parties. A killing fairly numbed him into a euphoria that lasted for days after which he experienced all the withdrawal symptoms associated with drug addiction. The thirst for adrenalin became all consuming. When he could not get out to the bush, he resided day and night in grass shacks that passed for bars in the company of prostitutes who supplied an equally potent although brief adrenalin rush. He missed inspections and duties and as a result suffered punishments. He was promoted many times and demoted just as often. These transgressions were always forgiven when Kluggmann took to the bush on patrol. There he shined in his duties like a diamond among mud clots. Even though this addiction ran his life, he never lost the shepherd's instinct. He often took the time to teach others his skills. Fellow soldiers marveled at his patience for teaching the inexperienced and constantly recommended him for awards and promotion which he lost at the first opportunity when idle in barracks. When war broke out between the Boers and British in the nearby Cape Colonies, the officers had sent Kluggmann to help train the Dutch farmers. He shot at Englishmen with as much gusto as he had potted at colony natives. He came back after the capture of the Boer capitals and was quickly sent off to help in the suppression of the Chinese Boxer Rebellion. There he had followed the Kaiser's orders and acted as a Hun would have. He could remember little of his service there as the killing, raping and pillaging kept him in an adrenalin stupor.

Now he was a shepherd again to a motley threesome who knew little of killing but was pliable. Liebermann, a man who had the ability of find food and luxuries in a waste land of trenches and shell holes, made sure that Kluggmann wanted for nothing even in times of local famine. He was loyal, trusting and very much like that dog that had taken to him in China. Until he had fallen in with this group, the dog had been the only entity he had confided his inner most thoughts to. Its death had traumatized Kluggmann to the point of suicide but the drug of adrenaline had brought him back from the edge. Kowalski, on the other hand, stimulated his mind with reasoning out the brutish nature of a soldier's existence. He gave Kluggmann rationality for the exhilaration he felt in killing. Lange was the son he may have had from any of the liaisons he had had in Asia or Africa. He felt that a strange bond of kinship existed between himself and Lange. What's more Lange supplied humor. His lankiness coupled with the ill fitting manner of his uniform reminded him of the small dolls the African natives made in the likeness of German soldiers. Some of the dolls were animated by pulling a string that ran up their backs. The string jerked the legs and arms into movements that resembled goose stepping, the favorite parade march of the colonial masters. Lange moved like those dolls and it tickled Kluggmann into laughter, something he had not done since that night in the grocery.

A shell burst in the hole they had just left bringing Kluggmann out of his reflection and into reality. 'Had we not evacuated it, we would have been killed,' Kluggmann thought to himself smirking when he asked himself if the movement had been luck. Mentally he answered the taunt. 'Nothing to do with luck. Just being a well trained soldier who understood the battlefield.'

Liebermann's helmet rolled between them and Kluggmann picked it up half expecting to find Liebermann's head in it. He was relieved and disappointed to find it empty. Liebermann jerked the helmet out of Kluggmann's hands and placed it back on his head. If Liebermann had a first name, no one knew it. Outside of the four, the rest of the company called him all sorts of names none of which were flattering until they needed food and water. They had nothing but praise for him then. He was always the first to volunteer to go back to the cook lines with a few other non-volunteers through artillery and machine gun barrages to retrieve the rations. In all of his trips he had never failed to return with his quarry and something additional that he shared out after he took a special cut. Yet, he had never returned with all the men of the ration carrying detail. After the feeding and watering, when the men were content they would take stock of who had not returned with Liebermann. Many times he had left with six men only to return as a sole survivor. That's when the name calling began again. Liebermann simply tucked his head between his shoulders and slinked off to sit with his three mates who rewarded him with parts of their meals. Kluggmann may have been an ogre in human garb but he was noble in Liebermann's eyes.

As for Kowalski, Liebermann, who had received a meager education on the Berlin streets, had nothing but praise for him. He never
tired of hearing Kowalski expound on topics which were beyond
Liebermann's simple intellect. He was in awe of what he saw as su-
per intelligence. It was the same with Lange whom he considered to
be a comrade of breeding since he came from the same Berlin streets
where he had been raised although from a richer side. Yet he saw
each of them as naïve in the art of survival. It seemed that among
the four only he understood the methods for obtaining things that
kept the soul with the body and dispelled the aches and pains of
daily life. But he was grateful for their tolerance. They looked beyond what he was to who he was.

In quick succession, four heavy caliber shells burst far behind the
foursome but close enough to shake them. The explosions were followed by a crescendo of seventy-five millimeter shells that spewed
shrapnel bullets all around. The brief fusillade landed on the company line instead of the sap and then shifted, in all its fury, to the
rear areas in an effort to prevent reserves from coming forward. The
four minds knew that the attack was coming. The shriek of a whistle
confirmed their suspicion. Kluggmann took off his gas mask as did
the others. The furious artillery fire had probably dissipated the gas
if there had been any in the first place. He then indicated in pantomime because the deafening noise negated words where each of
them should position themselves to repulse the attack or to receive
death. He put his rifle to his hip and grossly exaggerated the steps to
checking the magazine to see if it was loaded and the first shell was
in the breech. Everyone followed his example; they understood what
Kluggmann was saying. Kluggmann then leaned over to the wounded man to ask, again in gestures, whether he could still fire his rifle.
The man, a nameless man, nodded. Replacement soldiers came and
went so fast that Kluggmann never learned their names nor did he
try. Between the Old Folks, he referred to them as no-name soldiers.

MICHAEL P. KIHNTOPF

Kluggmann helped the wounded man to a firing position after making sure the rifle was loaded and the man had rounds to reload.

Slowly, the crescendo of humans yelling grew to dominate the sounds of the bursting artillery and staccato machine gun fire. The shouting and screaming was a primeval sound that men had used since time immemorial to strike fear into the opponents they meant to kill. The French were advancing at battalion strength but they were to the right of the sap. Kluggmann caught hold of his thoughts as they slowly succumbed to the thrill of danger and shot off the green flare. He readjusted everyone's firing position to pour fire into the advancing enemy's flank. He pointed to his rifle and himself to indicate that he would begin the shooting. There was a good possibility that the enemy might think that the artillery had destroyed the sap thus giving them a greater chance of survival and the advantage of surprise when they opened fire. The green flare's explosion didn't necessarily give away their position. The flare would come as a surprise and without a burning trail that lighter flares gave off, there would be no way of tracing it to its origins. He thought of the valiant effort he would put into the defense even though their miniscule fusillade could not hope to stop the attack. It could, however, blunt the stampeding horde's enthusiasm.

Seconds of hourly length passed and finally the enemy began to appear. The empty battlefield took on life and for a brief moment, the four were aghast to actually see the enemy. Men made of mud came forward as the tide to the shore; weakly at first and then as a surge. Groups of two or three swelled to hundreds who fell into shell holes or tripped over debris and rose again to continue the advance. Like the incoming water they bunched together at depressions seeking safety in numbers and flowed into areas where the going was easy. The leaders stood out because of a lack of rifle or, some pompous asses, because of a flashing sword raised high above the mob. Kluggmann aimed carefully at one of those sword brandishing men and squeezed off a round. The man fell as Kluggmann expected. He rarely missed. Four rifles spoke after his. He barely heard the shots of the others over the roar of adrenalin in his ears. Chambering another round he simply began firing at anyone as did his comrades. There were so many in such a solid mass that a single unaimed bullet could bring down two or three. The effect of their crashing rounds soon showed. The attacking groups swayed inward away from the source of fire like water moving into a channel of least resistance away from a protruding rock. Still they rushed on. The French rarely deviated from their objective keeping it firmly in sight and ignoring things that they had not factored into achieving their overall goal. The inexperienced officers viewed any deviation from the quickest path as a possible mutiny and dealt out summary executions in cold blood. Kluggmann's group continued to pour in rounds reloading the five bullet stripper clips automatically. Liebermann suspended his firing to take the ammunition out of the pouches of the dead men and distribute them to the shooters.

After a while, the French became painfully aware to the riflemen's pit to their left. A riding stick pointed at some men and then toward the sap. A group of ten broke off and moved directly for it. They took advantage of the slight rises hiding behind them to loose a few rounds. Kluggmann, not to be fooled by such an amateur action, could see that the ten were a decoy and another group was attempting to outflank their position. He jabbed Lange in the ribs and pointed to the flanking group. They both opened fire felling two but not before grenades were thrown. The bombs didn't reach the hole and exploded harmlessly a meter away. dust clouds rose obscuring the visions of all. Kluggmann motioned to Lange to cease fire and wait. The decoy group, thinking that the explosions had silenced their enemy, rose to rush what they hoped were stunned survivors. Lange and Kluggmann shot half of them down. Machine guns from the company line opened fire. The French mud men fell in tens and twenties. Soon the fire had its effect. The survivors turned to go back to the safety of their former positions. Officers tried to stop them with shouts and pistol shots whose bullets went over the heads of the retreating masses. There was nothing they could do to stop them. Death from in front or behind was the same. Where officers shot soldiers, soldiers shot officers. Seeing the destruction of their comrades and that the main body was retreating, the group that was trying to deal with the sap broke off the action and rejoined the masses. The French artillery brought its fire forward to bombard the strong resistance in preparation for a new advance. Many shells fell short among the retreaters. At the trenches, officers began rallying the men. Reserves were added to the depleted ranks. Kluggmann could see the rally points from the sap. He took note of the enemy's reforming locations and grabbed Liebermann by the collar. He indicated where the locations were and shouted in his ear.

"Go back to the company and tell them where the French are rallying. Come back with ammunition and water if it can be found!" Liebermann did not argue or hesitate. His master had given him a command and he wanted to please him. Carefully he placed his rifle to one side gave his spare cartridges to Lange and crawled over the crater's rim. The grey morning shielded him from observation although bullets kicked up dust around him. To bolster his courage, he assured himself that he had not been seen and that the bullets that came close were errant unaimed rounds. As Lange watched him crawl along he thought of a snake slithering across the ground.

Liebermann was a man with a mission but he was also a realist who saw opportunities to take advantage of while accomplishing his task. He reasoned that there was a possibility that he might not make it back to the company strong point just thirty meters away. He was dedicated to his goal but he was not such a fool as to brave deadly artillery concentrations or one to take on an enemy more determined then him. Such blockages would be understandable. Still, he reasoned, he had to complete his mission one way or another. To fulfill that aim he sought other resources. The Verdun battlefield was rarely policed of the dead. Bodies lay strewn about. Liebermann snaked his way through these corpses. Whenever he found a German corpse, he checked the ammunition pouches and the water bottles. He detached pouches containing bullets and carefully stacked them next to the corpses. He shook water bottles and placed those still containing liquid next to the pouches. Should he be unable to get to the company, he would collect those piles and return to the sap. What little there was obtained in that way was better than nothing. Finally, he reached the company line and found the person in charge. As stiffly as he could, he reported to his superior.

"I wish to report that Grenadier Liebermann brings news of the outpost." The lieutenant nodded. "We have four unwounded and one wounded with the rest dead or missing. We are in need of ammunition and water but we are holding." Then he told the lieutenant of the places where the enemy was rallying for a new assault. The lieutenant noted them and sent one of his own runners to alert the artillery to the new targets. Liebermann had stood riveted to the place from which he had first addressed the company commander but his eyes had wandered into every nook and cranny and his mind had taken note of any articles he could snatch as soon as he was released.

"Stand at ease, grenadier", the lieutenant shouted as he turned away from his dispatched runners. "I might have known you Old Folks would survive out there. I cannot relieve you as yet. Get what you need and return with the orders of hold until relieved. The French will mount another attack shortly and it may come to your location. They have seen that this position is too strong and they will probe for other weaknesses. Tell Kluggmann that we are depending on him. That's all." Liebermann went stiff again in salute turned and looked for ammunition. He found a box and took five belts out looping them over his neck. It was a heavy load for his scrawny neck but he endured it for the sake of his comrades. There was no water to be found. In less than fifteen minutes, he was again slithering across the ground to the sap. He had carefully marked his way so that he reached all the stacks of ammunition and water bottles he had skillfully placed. To make carrying easier, he had emptied a sandbag before leaving the strong point. Into that he placed the water bottles and loose ammunition. He did not neglect any French dead that he found along the way. Their water bottles often contained wine and Kluggmann was very fond of pinot rouge.

After an hour, Lieberman was back in the hole and distributing all that he had found and brought along. He told Kluggmann what the lieutenant had ordered. Kluggmann was delighted to comply. While Liebermann was gone, Kowalski had crawled to the party of Frenchmen that Lange and Kluggmann had killed. He had stripped the bodies of their water bottles and grenades. The sap was a well equipped and provisioned fort.

A barrage of seventy-fives announced that the next attack was coming. Kluggmann offered a drink of wine to everyone with a special portion to Liebermann who was most grateful. The wounded man was no longer an asset to the group. Although still alive, his face had become pasty white and he drifted between awareness and oblivion. Kluggmann offered him some of the wine. He clutched at the bottle as if it offered a cure for his wounds. After the drink he smiled and pushed his rifle to Kluggmann shaking his head. He was unable to even lift the weapon. Kluggmann knew that the man was resigning himself from any more of the defense. Blood had already saturated the bandages Liebermann had put on him. Kluggmann nodded and signed that the others should spread out to cover the wounded man's position. Kowalski then took the injured man further down into the shell crater away from the rim. The seventy-fives' barrage was punctuated by heavier calibers but still the shells fell on the company positions and not the sap.

Lange raised his hand to get Kluggmann's attention and then pointed to the right. All understood that the enemy was coming their way. The four of them crouched as close to the rim of the hole as they could. Invariably, the attackers would hurdle their grenades into the hole but the floor was not flat. The bombs would tumble down the walls to the bottom. The rim was the safest place. No one made an effort to retrieve the wounded man. They understood that he would be dead anyway in a few moments because of the loss of blood. In seconds the black objects, like large stones, came arcing in from the front and right. They tumbled down the hole's sloping sides to the puddle at the bottom or were stopped by the wounded man whose eyes could only pop. His limbs were useless. He couldn't push them away. The grenades' explosions were absorbed by the water at the hole's bottom and the wounded man's body. There was a shout and six men jumped into the hole. Kluggmann speared one with his bayoneted rifle and Lange shot another. Kowalski wrestled the bayoneted rifle out of his attacker's hands and crushed his skull with the Frenchman's own rifle butt. Liebermann took a pistol from his pocket and shot one in the face and another in the stomach. The survivor, on seeing his comrades so swiftly dispatched threw up his hands. He was shot three times. The man who had been shot in the stomach was also finished off with a bullet to the head. The bodies were pushed to the bottom where they joined the once wounded man's remains. Firing positions were resumed in time to see that the wave was coming in their direction. The one brain thought up the reaction. Half the body went to the left while the other half went to the rear. A cross fire was set up over an area of ten meters. Lange began throwing the captured French grenades which caused confusion in the charging ranks. They did not return fire because they recognized the explosions to be their own ordinance. Thinking that their advance party had put the enemy in the sap to rest they were confused. They called out that the group should stop firing on their own men. When the Mauser bullets began tearing into their ranks, they understood and leapt forward to be met by arcing machine gun fire. The company had repositioned the machine guns to support the outpost. The fire was devastating. The Old Folks added to the mayhem with their bullets. The attack broke down although the left of the company line appeared to have been breached. The two halves of the brain reunited in the center of the hole and congratu-lated themselves on having survived. Kluggmann was as cheery as a schoolboy on a field trip. The adrenaline made him roar out encour-agement and award mighty back slaps to all. However, ammunition was very low. Liebermann pointed out that soon they would have only a bayonet with which to fight. As one they made a decision. Go back to the company.

Chapter 2
0600 - 0900

"I didn't expect you to come back after the orders I gave you," said Lieutenant Pfeiffer when he saw Kluggmann coming through the communication trench toward him. The lieutenant was just coming back from assessing the company's losses as a result of the recent attack. There had been ten killed by the artillery before the main attack and three wounded thereafter, again, by cannon fire. He indulged himself in self-congratulations, before Kluggmann could answer him, on having few casualties during the assault as a result of small arms fire. Battalion would also give praise for the low loss rate. They forgave deaths by artillery fire as attritional losses which the lieutenant's training methods could not have precluded. The success of his training record showed on how well his men had responded to a few of the enemy getting into the trench on the left. His men had bombed them to death or caused them to surrender before they could get into the main network. There had been no casualties in that fracas. Additionally, the machine guns, under his direction, had repelled the rest of the attackers before they could reinforce their comrades. It was a fine coup de main that should get into his records and possibly lead to some kind of recognition.

"I wish to report that the outpost ran out of ammunition and men, Herr Lieutenant," Kluggmann said while standing as relaxed as he could to show his dislike for the company commander. Pfeiffer was Kluggmann's seventh company commander since he had been assigned to the front lines. Enemy fire had killed four while the other two had suffered severe wounds necessitating evacuation. Kluggmann saw no future in respecting the officers in charge if they were so quick to get themselves taken out of the battle. They were not the fighting sort he had been use to in Africa. Those officers led from the front but took cover when the going got tough. They were not too proud to show fear. As a result, they lasted longer in the leadership role. Kluggmann often complained to himself that Pfeiffer was not of the old caste, the real officers who knew how to command men through respect and aloofness. Pfeiffer's appearance said it all to Kluggmann. The lieutenant's uniform was too neat. He took care to brush off mud and mend lost buttons. Clearly he used the uniform to hide his origins. He was from the working class, a factory man with dirty hands now scrupulously clean. He marked down Pfeiffer as a candidate for the insane asylum. Too neat and orderly and too sensitive to his own needs in pursuing those interests. He had heard of such officers as having lost their minds when pressure destroyed their orderly world. They froze, couldn't speak, or just wandered off never to be seen or heard from again. Some even cried themselves into unconsciousness or screamed senseless orders that no one would or could follow. The signs were there. He was too meticulous. How many times had he told the men that everything had its place, function, and time? Pfeiffer preferred to have a plan for everything. That was a fool's objective. War was chaos in which plans evaporated after the first shots. Napoleon had said something like that a hundred years before.

The gefreiter's inappropriate posture was not missed by Pfeiffer but he did not correct it in the normal Prussian way. He had learned in the short time of his command that Kluggmann was a dyed in the wool professional soldier and felt no sting in confinement, fines, or extra work details. Pfeiffer's plan was to chastise through sarcasm, a few choice words which gnawed at the gefreiter's immense ego. He had trained a dog using such methods.

"But you had your bayonet, Kluggmann. All that service in Africa, surely you learned how to use a spear?" He paused to see if the words had any effect. There wasn't so much as a blink. He felt a little defeated. "Never mind, we have been relieved anyway." He paused for a moment, assessing the situation. In the distance he could see a man standing outside his bunker. It was probably Braun coming to assume the position with the other half of the company that had been held in reserve. The sight of such a respectful man as Vizefeldwebel Braun, all spit and polish, gave inspiration. He turned back to Kluggmann. "It's all just as well. I would have had to send someone out to get your lot. So, your dereliction to orders probably saved that man." With a smirk on his face, which Kluggmann did not see because he kept his eyes riveted to the trench's floor, he added. "Or maybe I would have assumed that you were all killed and couldn't be recalled. How many have you brought back?"

"I beg to report that there are four of us left."

"Are any of them the new men I assigned to your section?" Kluggmann shook his head. Pfeiffer's congratulatory mood evaporated. "I should have guessed. How is it you four always survive while the others always die or disappear? Don't answer. I know. It's the training that the poor sods get now-a-days back at the barracks that kills them. It's not a reflection of the training you give them. It's my neck that's on the block. I'm responsible for those lost whether I arrived in '14 or yesterday. The loss of your four men has blemished my record, Kluggmann, but you go on without blame." Pfeiffer noted an eye blink. He congratulated himself as having scored a blow. "Or do you?" Another blink and this time a dropping of the head to match. "How did they die?"

"I am grieved to report that three were killed by artillery and one by a grenade." Pfeiffer almost smiled. His record of few casualties had not suffered much with the loss of those men. He turned to walk away and then looked over his shoulder. He had thought of another biting comment to add to that already heaped on which might put Kluggmann in his place but in his zeal to deliver that sarcasm he made the mistake of straightening up a little too much. A sniper's bullet smashed into the trench wall narrowly missing his head. He immediately forgot the comment, crouched low and continued walking toward Braun. His pace was even and unrushed. He did not want to appear to be afraid or running. That would be embarrassing. Even though he wanted to stop himself from doing it, he waved and hollered at Braun. He wanted to show Kluggmann that he had no personal fear for his life. It was all part of exercising a personal control he had learned from one of the old breed of officers.

Pfeiffer had been a volunteer to the military at seventeen, a candidate for a reserve officer, long before the current war. During one of the evaluation periods, a crusty old hauptman had confided in him that officers should develop a disposition where they had two faces. One face that showed indifference to danger and petty insubordination and another inner face that screamed at disobedience and trembled when danger was near. Above all else, the hauptman had told him, the inner face had to be hidden. Had he been able to see Pfeiffer's face, Kluggmann would have seen a cool, nonchalant expression. His pace in leaving the area relayed that just as well. Kluggmann took note of Pfeiffer's attitude and went to find his things and his comrades. Inwardly, he mulled over the sniper's near miss.

'Almost got him that time. He showed good pluck though. Didn't bat an eyelash and just turned to do his duty,' Kluggmann thought. Then the news sunk in. "Relieved! Again!" he shouted out loud. The soldier standing watch close by let out a contented sigh. Kluggmann, after sizing up the soldier from foot to head, patted him on the back. "Don't fret, comrade, I know how you feel. We just get involved in action and someone thinks we've had enough after just a few deaths. I tell you, I feel like I'm not earning my pay on days like this." The soldier was dumbfounded and showed it in his expression.

The French artillery barrage was intensifying again but the explosions were in the reserve trenches. 'Another assault soon,' Kluggmann thought. 'This time we won't be as lucky.' He knew where his comrades would be. The large dugout was where they kept the food and water. Liebermann would have led them there.

"I wish to report to the Lieutenant that we had a lot of casualties on the way here," said the Vizefeldwebel Braun as Pfeiffer approached. Braun started to straighten his posture but Pfeiffer motioned for him to keep his head down.

"There's a sniper out there that has the range of this part of the trench. Don't show your tete above the rampart. What happened?"

"A sudden machine gun barrage at the open area before entering the communications trench caught us and we lost nine men, three killed outright. I've sent the wounded that could walk back. We had to leave two there at the trench entrance. I didn't want to spare the men to take them back. Could some of your men pick them up on the way back and get them to an aid station if they are still alive?" Pfeiffer nodded. Inside he raged. He knew there was no use taking it out on Braun. The vizefeldwebel wasn't at fault. He had done the right thing in sticking to the relief schedule but he shouldn't have laid the responsibility of additional wounded men on him. Braun should have realized, Pfeiffer thought, that the outgoing half company would have their own wounded to deal with. Braun continued, "Can you spare any men who haven't been too terribly taxed since you've been up here? I'll only need them until we get settled in and I can see how best to cover the gaps."

"We are all pretty well spent. The Frenchies kept counterattacking in battalion strength along here yesterday and this morning. We just beat two waves back." He paused to assess the reaction on Braun's face. Braun's eyes grew rounder. Braun was not a brave man but he was resourceful and that was what got him his rank. Before the war he had been a supply sergeant now he commanded a half company. "But, I have just the men for you." Lange was just passing him. Pfeiffer reached out catching the grenadier by the collar. Lange looked like a puppy whose mother had just picked him up by the nape. "Tell your section that they are to report here to this vizefeldwebel for orders. He will assume command of your section until he feels confident that he can release you."

"But sir, there is only four of us left," protested Lange.

"Never mind that! Follow orders!" He released Lange and gave him a little shove down the communicator trench. Unconsciously Pfeiffer took out his watch. Before the war he had managed a machine shop. He had always noted the time when he gave the workers instructions for the day. It was a habit that had saved his job often. By knowing the time he could point out that he had set goals at such and such a time but the foremen had not released those instructions to their workers in a timely manner. Any faults for not meeting quotas fell on the foremen and not him. When he pushed the round button on the watch's side to uncover the dial a light airy tune drifted to his ears. Despite the constant din of exploding shells and chattering machine guns he seemed to always hear the melody. It reminded him of his niece who had given him the watch. She had been so beautiful before her marriage and so devoted to him. But the man she married had been a brute who beat her. One of the beatings had been too much and the girl had died. Pfeiffer had been furious and hired two thugs to get revenge. The niece's husband had disappeared one day never to be seen or heard from again. Most thought he had run off to avoid any vengeance but Pfeiffer knew better. The watch showed that it was six. Daylight was visible but the lower half of the terrain shielded by low hills was still hidden in darkness. Getting back to the reserve area had to be done quickly before daylight showed the movement. For an instance, he thought of the curtain of exploding shells or, according to Braun, the machine gun barrage that separated the front from the deep bunkers of the reserve positions. It seemed strange that the front line was safer than the route he was about to take. He turned to Braun. "We have to be going now. Good luck."

Lange found Kluggmann and the rest squatting near a fire. Fires, those that warmed the hands and butt, were allowed in the early morning when the fog hid the smoke. The French also had fires at that time but theirs were for cooking. The aromas that drifted across no mans' land attested to their activity. Such heavenly smells they were. Some said the French still had real coffee, from their colonies. It was hard to stomach the weak hazelnut coffee that was served with black bread when those odors wafted through the air. When Lange told his section of the orders, Kluggmann was delighted while the others resigned themselves to their fate. Only Lange was unsettled in what he should think. Youth often lacks the experience that is needed to arrive at a firm decision; however, his immediate concern was food. Liebermann had located the rations carriers before they had reached the rest of the company to distribute their bounty. He managed to get his section's portion of the bread and coffee neglecting to mention that half his section had been killed. He even managed to trade an artillery shell's driving ring to one of the carriers for extra tobacco for Kowalski. Liebermann had not made the transaction because he was thoughtful toward his comrade in arms. He knew that Kowalski would first light up and smoke before eating because of his addiction to the weed. The tobacco stunted Kowalski's appetite and he would eat less. Liebermann would then use the leftovers as trading material among the less fortunate. Maybe he could even get back the driving ring. As they gorged themselves on double rations, all four decided that since the Lieutenant had only said report to the new commander and didn't specify a time that they could sit for a while to digest their food maybe take a nap on a full stomach. The options for putting off reporting were boundless.

With his mouth full of dark bread, Kluggmann leaned over to Lange who chewed laboriously. "You know that Lieutenant isn't so bad after all. I thought he didn't like me, not that I cared. Now I see that he's just being formal in that Prussian sort of way." He paused to think of something nice to say about Pfeiffer. It was hard but then he remembered the near miss that had garnered his appreciation. "You should have seen how cool and calm he was when some sniper missed him by only a few centimeters. It was so close that the dirt that the bullet turned out from the trench wall must have hit him in the eye. Know what he did?" Lange was more concerned about breaking the bread into mush before he swallowed the mouthful he had committed to. He did manage a shrug and a small grunt in answer to the question. Kluggmann, rapped in his own imagery, didn't notice the shrug or hear the grunt. "He just shrugged it off like a professional. Wow! You know, one of the old breed must have trained him. But mark my words, that bravado will be his undoing." Kluggmann stopped his conversation to give Lange a few hard pats on the back. The bread had gotten stuck in Lange's throat and he was turning blue. The lump went down and Lange gasped for air. "You got to chew more no matter how hungry you are. That stuff's made with turnips and sawdust, you know that. Even a termite can't swallow it in large lumps like you want to." Kluggmann's eyes took on a contemplative look as he returned to his original thought. "One day, after many near misses, he'll think that he's charmed and then..." Kluggmann finished the sentence by drawing his fingers across his throat. Lange grimaced more because he was thinking about another bit of the bread than Kluggmann's warning. The enemy's barrage was beginning to drown out any other sounds. Kluggmann rose stuffing the remainders of his army loaf into his pant pocket and shouted, "Looks like the shop just opened. Let's go see what we can do for this vizefeldwebel." Kowalski had already dropped off to sleep and was beginning to snore. For a few seconds, Kluggmann stood over him admiring the fact that Kowalski could fall asleep anywhere at any time then he kicked the soles of his boots. "Will you join us, dear Gretel?" Kluggmann said while bowing like a school boy with one arm bent at his waist and one arm behind him.

At the dugout, the vizefeldwebel sighed. Inwardly, Braun registered compassion for the four men who had been fighting for the last five days and nights but he didn't show it. Instead, he outwardly showed his disdain for having received the Old Folks as fillers to his already depleted and demoralized ranks. The men would take this as a sign that they were doomed. "Does your lieutenant have it out for you lot?" he asked Kluggmann who was about to answer but was cut off. "No reply is necessary. Take your section and reinforce my first platoon's second section. They're on the right near the end of the trench line." Bursting shrapnel shells drowned out what was said next and Kluggmann cupped his hand around his ear to indicate that he had not heard the rest of the instructions. Braun stopped himself from speaking and waited until the din subsided for the rest of the speech. "I'm counting on your section to bolster those men. They're green." Kluggmann nodded. The Old Folks trotted off calling for the second section. They went as far as the trench would allow but there was no answer to their summons. Kowalski waited until there was a brief interlude between shell bursts and called out again for the second section. His call worked and there was a hail from some shell holes a little forward of the line's end.

"Why is it that we always get the shallow end of the line?" Liebermann asked of no one in particular. All four crawled out of the trench to the first shell hole where they found Sergeant Koblenz and seven of his men. Kluggmann told the sergeant that they were there to help out. Koblenz winced. His men wouldn't like working with the Old Folks. Two who were near enough to hear Kluggmann groaned and crossed themselves. Nevertheless, Koblenz set them to work.

The four of them, assisted by the new second section, spent the next two hours providing for their own safety. They deepened and connected the shell holes they called a trench. After they had done that they were to dig a connection to the main trench. Often, in their digging, they came across a corpse or a body part. The new soldiers grimaced and stared while Liebermann simply picked up the putrefied pieces and threw them in one direction or the other depending on which way the wind was blowing. He cautioned those new recruits about throwing body parts in just any direction. Should they make an error and throw it in the wrong direction, the wind would bring the smell of rotten flesh to them all day and all night. Eventually it happened. They dug into a whole decomposing body invested with baby rats who squealed in protest of having their meal interrupted. A few adult rats were also present but quickly ran off leaving the small ones to their fate, the flats of the workers' shovels. Mayhem done, Liebermann had to coax the men into helping him get the body out of the way. He place two men on the legs cautioning them to lift at the thighs and then assisted another man at the chest. With a count to three, all four men lifted the corpse and threw it as far away as possible. Everyone dusted everyone else off making sure no maggots remained. A rest would have been in order but a machine gun began firing at the corpse and the rim of the hole they were in. The splattering bullets reminded them how shallow their protection was. They went back to digging.

Another corpse soon came to light. Liebermann feigned a muscle cramp in his back adding that he had shown them how to deal with the body. He sat down to enjoy his favorite joke with new people. He looked away gauging how much more work had to be done. New people never follow the instructions or examples of those who have been in the trenches longer. New people always know a better way to get things done. Instead of positioning themselves at the chest and thighs, they decided to grab the arms and legs and heft the corpse out. The result was always the same; the appendages just broke off in their hands. One threw the limb he pulled off away in disgust while two of the others simply stared at what they had in hand unable to throw the limb away. Their eyes became as big as saucer plates and their mouths dropped open; then came the usual curses and stammering. Liebermann laughed uproariously inside. He loved the expressions on their faces. He shook his head and his face took on a disgusted look as he cursed the men.

"You clods! Now you've done it. Throw that stuff away and pick the body up like I showed you. Just think. Some poor wife or mother put a lot of effort into forming that body and you go and pull it apart like it's a doll. I should make each one of you write a letter to the next of kin apologizing for your behavior. No. Better yet. I think you should think about yourselves. Who's going to dig you up one day and treat you the same way. "

Kowalski stood watch. The others could dig, he said to himself. That was the type of work he had hoped to avoid while he was in the army. Get someone else to do it; that was his motto. The enemy's barrage was still heavy but it fell on the rear areas. He wondered how many casualties the Lieutenant would have before he reached the safety of the deep dugouts that were so well concealed among the fallen trees of the once flourishing forest that had been here. Kowalski studied the explosions from his position. It appeared that they formed a curtain from the cascading earth mixed with tons of steel. The fire that the bursts released gave the earthly torrent a shimmering affect. Where had he seen such a scene before? Then he remembered the stage curtain at the cheap theater he had liked to attend before the war. The drapery had once been a vivid red with black interwoven in an East Indian pattern but the years of neglect had taken their toll and the reds had changed to browns and in a multitude of places moth holes allowed the backstage lighting to peep through. He could see that curtain as if he were sitting in front of it waiting for the play to begin. He shook his head as if that motion would dispel his daydream. For a moment he saw again the blowing dirt and shell explosions but the curtain dream came back. He shook his head again. Why had he thought of that theater? In response to the shaking, the memory grabbed a hold of him with steel tipped mental talons in an effort to stay alive in his thoughts for a fraction of time longer.

It was a vivid vision. He could hear the murmuring of the audience as it seated itself around him. He always arrived early. The large room was preferable to his attic apartment that only allowed him three or four paces of space. Many of the audience were critics even before the entertainment began. They commented on the program printed on cheap butcher's paper, the lighting which was still gas, and on any other thing that they saw as archaic or not up to modern standards. There was always a comment about the brocaded brown seats that were threadbare. Many had springs that protruded above the fabric. Woe on a patron who did not feel the cushion before sitting. Cleanliness was always a source of discussion too. For a second Kowalski could smell the dust that had accumulated on the stage and on the floor in the lesser used sections. It was not a big place. Maybe one hundred could fit in at one time. Personally, he had never seen more than twenty-five or thirty patrons which meant that there were large areas that had gone neglected by the charwoman. The cleaning staff, in reaction to their meager wages, chose to sweep only those areas that definitely showed signs of use leaving the traditionally vacant areas alone.

Nevertheless, Kowalski was proud of the place in his own way because it risked being shut down by the censors every once in a while by presenting political plays that were critical of the Kaiser's ministers. Those plays were never announced, naturally. One had to be one of the trusted acceptable clients who frequented the house to receive notice of such shows. The announcement was normally a whisper by the usher in the patron's ear as he left a sanctioned performance. Perhaps, he continued to fanaticize, after the war was over, he could get more involved in those risqué productions and the politics they came from. He was already a member of the socialist party in good standing through his union. He had paid his union dues through 1917 to remain on their roles. The war couldn't last longer than that.

An aeroplane turned lazy loops above Kowalski's head and his gaze changed from the stage curtain to the plane. The machine drew fascinating circles among the clouds that were forming as the sun slowly rose. Was it friend or foe? He strained his eyes but could not make out the markings. A machine gun rattled and he watched the tracer bullets arc well below the aircraft. He cursed the fool who gave the machine gun's position away should the plane be the enemy. The machine did not interrupt its lazy circles which seemed to hypnotize him. They were so relaxing to follow. The monotonous actions coupled with the lack of sleep over the last five days and nights soon had Kowalski's eyes drooping. He cautioned himself that he mustn't fall asleep but his eyelids could barely hold themselves up. He stamped his feet and beat his shoulders. For a few minutes he felt revived. Then the fatigue began to set in with renewed vigor. His chin dropped to his chest. He snapped his head back. He was reminded of the flag that the starter whipped up in the air to start a horse race.

As if on cue, things changed. Only one shell burst in the curtain Kowalski had been watching. He stiffened to see what was wrong; fatigue forgotten. He watched as the dirt, constantly turned up by the exploding shells fell to earth in an audible crash reminiscent of a train crash. The ground shuttered with the return of its weight.

Lange shouted. "Cover!" And with the last syllable, a curtain of fire descended on the holes they were in. There was nothing to do but curl up into a ball and hope to survive. Blackness closed in around Liebermann as the nearby, blown up earth descended on him. He was safe in his fetal position covered by dirt for the time being. The earth was loose. There had been no heavy beams or sheets of iron to fall in on him as there would have been if he had been in a bunker. He poked his fingers through the dirt to give him a little breathing tube. The barrage lasted only a few seconds and shifted to the right. Kluggmann rose to his knees shaking off the dirt that had covered him. Lange did the same and noted in his first visions of the turned up world that the section sergeant was dead along with three other men. No wounded could be seen. Kluggmann was in charge again. The barrage shifted to the rear lines.

"Get ready!" Kluggmann shouted. Bolts rasped chambering the first rounds. Supporting machine guns began to clatter. But the only noise was that of exploding artillery. Minutes passed without the enemy showing himself. Tens of minutes passed. Still no rushing mob.

"See anything?" called one of the nameless soldiers, a survivor of the section. No one answered. The dawn had changed to full light and everyone looked in all directions for some kind of activity. Eyes squinted. Hands were put to ears. Nothing, except the detonations in the reserve trenches. Lange slipped in next to Kluggmann.

"Well?" Lange asked as if he were disappointed that an attack didn't follow the brief barrage.

"Sometimes they don't attack. Just want to size us up. Get us moving around so that guy in the flying machine can see how many are here." The plane still made lazy circles in the sky as if the brief cannonade had nothing to do with his war. The circles became smaller and then the plane dove down toward the ground. Lange and Kluggmann watched as the craft changed from a toy size to its reality image as if mesmerized. It appeared to be headed directly for their position. The markings showed it was French. Lange attempted to jump up in an effort to escape but Kluggmann pushed him back down against the trench's wall. His big miner's hand pushed hard on the shoulder to keep Lange in place. Two of the nameless soldiers had no one to watch over them. They left their protection and ran toward the rest of their company which was sheltered in a deeper trench. Machine gun fire from above cut them down. The plane swooped by and began to climb. Kluggmann and Lange fired after it knowing that their bullets would never reach any target. It was a matter of tit for tat. To their surprise, the plane exploded. They stopped firing and stared at one another in disbelief. Then the sounds of a heavy throated Maxim came to their ears. They looked up to see a German kampfflieger soar past them. The pilot rocked his craft and waved. The sound of the Maxim had been his guns delayed in reaching their ears by distance. There was a cheer from the company's positions. Kluggmann turned to Lange. "I guess we do have an effective air force after all. Someone deserves a medal for that one." To the rear, Lange noted movement coming their way.

"Braun is coming out to inspect," said Lange pointing to Braun's supply sergeant's hulk heaving itself out of the trench.

"The silly jackass", Kluggmann snorted. "Always so efficient. He's coming out to see how many are to be buried instead of making ready for an attack." He waved his hand above his head to get Braun's attention. "Go back!" he shouted to Braun. "There's six dead here with no wounded or missing. Koblenz is dead and I am assuming command." Braun froze to listen. He cupped his hand to his ear and Kluggmann repeated his message. Braun nodded and turned to get back to the trench. A machine gun spoke and the ground around Braun rose in small explosions and passed on. Braun did not move.

Kowalski thought out loud. "The sod's had it. He was always such a conscientious bastard, always checking on others without worrying about himself. Tsk, Tsk. He will be missed." Kowalski's voice reeked with sarcasm. As if in reaction to Kowalski's eulogy, Braun moved. Rising to an almost erect posture, he ran to the protecting trench before him diving into it as another machine gun opened fire on the spot he had left.

"Never saw him move so fast", Lange shouted gleefully. "He must have made those two meters in less than a second. Got luck behind him, I must say." Kowalski was open mouthed. Kluggmann broke up the impromptu admiration society.

"Pay attention. Watch for the enemy." Everyone went back to their position to wait but no one came. After half an hour, Kluggmann gave the command, "Stand down." He pointed to the two no-name soldiers. "You guys take up watch from Liebermann and Kowalski. I think the holes are connected well enough. Liebermann and Kowalski can begin cutting a communicator with the main trench. Lange, you go find out what's on our right flank. The Bavarians are supposed to be out there somewhere but how far?" Everyone got busy as the artillery continued.

Chapter 3

0900 – 1200

Liebermann noted that Kowalski let out a curse every time he brought his short handled pick down to gouge the earth. It was as if he was beating someone senseless and uttering a curse of revenge after every downward stroke. Kowalski had the job of breaking the ground up after which he would move aside and let Liebermann shovel the loose dirt away. The ground had been soft for the first foot but beneath the centuries of carefully nurtured farmer's soil lay eons of nature's unyielding, impacted clay. What made the task even more difficult was the posture the two had to take until they reached a depth that would shield them from death. At first they worked lying down, digging a type of sunken pathway. As they deepened the crawl space, they could rise to their knees but they still couldn't get a full swing at the earth. If Kowalski brought his pick too far up bullets from either a sniper or machine gun marksman followed. Once, a bullet had hit the pick sending it tumbling end on end beyond reach. Kowalski said it was a bad omen and that all digging should stop until a favorable sign came along. Kluggmann said that he was the favorable sign and that digging should continue. Kowalski didn't protest citing that it was his lot to be exploited by petty tyranny. Kluggmann smiled and agreed with him. Eventually Kowalski managed to take the sling off his rifle, make a loop and lasso the pick. His attempt to beat the ground to death began again.

It was clear to Liebermann that his mate did not enjoy the work but, for that matter, neither did he. The job became tedious to Liebermann but he managed to set a rhythm. Kowalski would hack, curse, hack, curse and then Liebermann would push him aside to shovel the loose soil away. He would throw two maybe three shovels full of earth on the parapet and then he would push Kowalski back to gouge. Hack, curse, hack, curse, push, shovel, shovel, shovel, push. In his mind's eye Liebermann envisioned the time he had learned to waltz. The artillery dissonance faded into the melodic music of Strauss. Hack, curse, hack, curse, push, shovel, shovel, shovel, push. Many of his street associates had said that he was mad to spend good money on such a frivolous endeavor as dancing. But there was method to his madness. Hack, curse, hack, curse, push, shovel, shovel, shovel, push.

He could see the tiled dance floor at the café he frequented. It was a checker board pattern of green and grey. The colors were discernible only to people who had frequented the place over the years. To the new customers, many of the green tiles had become grey and the grey had become greyer tinged with black until the floor had resembled one large tile with varying shades of grey. Surrounding the dance floor were pedestal tables covered in shabby linen at which dowagers on velvet upholstered chairs sat bespangled in glass jewels and smelling of sweat and sweet perfumes. They drank oceans of champagne cocktails becoming a little louder after each reorder. Their bosoms, enlarged by age and enhanced by a flower or bit of lace stuck rakishly in their cleavages, were perched on the table as melons would be at a farmer's stall. Their asses barely fit within the confines of the chairs arms that framed the seat cushion. They often shifted their weight on the poor cushion from one cheek to the other in an effort to get comfortable. Some slipped their bloated feet in and out of their shoes in an effort to relieve the pressure that too small shoes had on their aged corns. Liebermann found them attractive. He was not perverse; he found them attractive because they had either survived their wealthy husbands or had spouses who found younger women more attractive than them. They had the allure of money.

Liebermann, well-schooled in all the latest and passé dances, had become a vulture preying on these women who craved male companionship and had the money to pay for it. The waltz lessons paid for themselves within weeks as the women, grateful for his attentions and enamored with his agile movements, stuffed money in his pockets or gave him expensive gifts as he twirled them across the dance floor. In passing he gave these denizens of the dark club credit for being both spry and youthfully lithe despite the weight that some of them possessed. But he was a diplomat also. When a dance partner might falter on the floor because of too many cocktails, Liebermann cursed the swelling of the floor or a shift in rhythm. That play always brought him bigger tips. It was true that Liebermann didn't get to keep all the money, a percentage went to the café management, but what he did keep was substantial. He bought clothes that made him look more debonair and hid the fact that he was from the street gutters. He bought perfumes that were not too strong but enticing enough to blind the senses. The gifts he did not share. Rings, watches, fine leather straps all enhanced his image. The excess to his needs was quickly sold off. Hack, curse, hack, curse, push, shovel, shovel, shovel, push. The image grew stronger. Strauss's music grew louder accented by booming kettle drums. He swayed to the imagined music. A loud voice interrupted.

"Here! What are you playing at?" Kowalski shouted. Liebermann's dream snapped away. He looked around to see Kowalski at the bottom of the shell hole instead of in front of him hacking away. All around artillery shells were bursting sending out clouds of shrapnel bullets. The French had seen them and called in a barge since neither sniper nor machine guns could dislodge the diggers. Liebermann threw himself down into the shallow crawl trench.

The barrage lasted thirty seconds but failed to do anything more then fling bullets over the landscape. The French gunners were using shrapnel loads instead of high explosive loads which would have destroyed the breast works and exposed their enemy. They had apparently hoped that exploding the shells above ground would cause the bullets to reach into the trench depths. They didn't to any success.

Kluggmann was still cautioning his flock to watch for the assault. It was bound to come at any minute. Lange had returned to report that the Bavarians were firmly in place to the right nearly one hundred meters away but there was no easy way to get to them. The landscape was flat and open with only a few rises that could be used for cover and because of the spring rains; it was a sea of liquid mud nearly shins deep. The Bavarians were happy to know that their flank was not exposed and they could rely on the Prussians for support. Like Kluggmann's group they occupied shell holes rather than a network of deep trenches. The Bavarians thought it impossible to connect their works with the Prussians' because of the liquidness of the terrain separating them. The result was that there was a gap between companies. During daylight hours sentries could easily guard it but in the dark, one hundred meters was as wide as the Rhine. Hundreds of quiet men could easily slip into the gap and either attack the Bavarians or Kluggmann's position from the flank. Lange had suggested that the two elements could cooperate in setting up a crossfire zone to eliminate infiltration. The trick would be to keep from shooting each other. Kluggmann placed the no-name soldiers to cover the area cautioning them to keep their aim low. If there was any attempt at infiltration the men would crawl. A low aim had a better chance of hitting someone whereas a high aim would hit the Bavarians. Lange took up position next to Kluggmann to stare out across the scarred landscape. Lange was becoming impatient. Impatience led to frustration and frustration led to daydreaming. What was his fate? How would he die?

Death by the unknowing hand of artillery was not what Lange had envisioned war to be. He had started the war with images of Leonidas and his Spartans holding the line against the invader, dying nobly against overwhelming odds; but the experiences of the last months had shown him what war was. It was endless inactivity bracketed by indiscriminate killing by munitions that fell from on high propelled by an unseen enemy. The enemy was nowhere to be seen. His vision of a gallant and glorious death in hand to hand combat was shattered in the first artillery bombardment. Explosions rained from the sky tearing men who had not even fired one shot into pieces. Some of the mutilated masses were still alive and were carted off to doctors who reveled in saving the life regardless of the state of the body. It was then that he hoped for a quick death for himself. But then again, a lingering wound, one that he could recover from but not sufficiently to return to the trenches, might be to his advantage. A melancholic sigh often accompanied those thoughts. Clean white sheets. He thought of lying in starched white sheets in a clean ward. A gentle, cool breeze coming from the new mown fields would part the window's curtains. Sitting beside him would be Elsa, his one true love. Her ginger hair would lay loose on her fragile shoulders in marvelous drifts. She would listen attentively to his every word; clasp his hand lovingly while whispering of her undying love. She would even slip her hands under the sheets when no one was looking.

Kluggmann's rifle spoke. Amid the shell explosions, the Mauser's bang sounded like the report of a child's cork shooting gun, nevertheless, it brought about a chorus from the other rifles in the shell hole. Everyone fired and then looked to see what they were shooting at. Kluggmann rolled over to his back, ejected the spent round, and glared at everyone.

"Can't a guy just shoot?" he yelled. "I saw something and pulled the trigger. If I wanted your help, I would have asked. Go back to what you were doing." Hack, curse, hack, curse, push, shovel, shovel, shovel, push.

By eleven, Liebermann and Kowalski had managed to reach half way to the main trench. The communicator was a meter wide and deep crawl. The dirt they had dislodged to get the shallow trench provided an additional meter of height but it was not protection. The soil was still loose and would not stop any bullets until it had been firmly packed down and reinforced. They would have to do that at night when they could crawl out of the trench in relative safety to tamp the outside that faced the enemy. Kluggmann and the rest surmised that Braun had ordered the men at his end to work toward Kluggmann's position. The gap between the two groups was narrowing. Kowalski was losing his timing as any good worker should have. Internally, he questioned why he should work so hard. He went on to reason, in his strictly practical way, that those coming towards him should be allotted the pleasure of digging the most. It would bolster their morale to be the ones to break through to the poor beleaguered group. He envisioned future stories about a lost section that was saved by the dauntless efforts of a few which did not include him. The tale might even make the trench newspaper and filter back to Germany's press. Between hacking and cursing, Kowalski injected a sigh of contentment. Liebermann lost the tempo for a bit and involuntarily cursed the band leader.

Kowalski made a prophetic observation to no one in particular, during one of the shovel, shovel, shovel, push periods, "You know I like the solitude of these forward, disconnected positions. No one bothers us out here. We support one another as the need arises and don't put on airs about being vigilant when we can barely keep our eyes open." The other Old Folks nodded in agreement. A dreamy state crossed their faces showing that they remembered a time when they were their own masters and not the slaves of the hierarchy of officers and non-commissioned officers. The no-name soldiers could only muster quizzical looks. "When we get connected with those others, Braun will be out here every other hour to make sure we are doing the soldierly thing and he will be setting watch schedules and duty details. We won't be able to even think of a brief rest now and then or a smoke break when the need arises. I wish there was some way to slow those guys down a little." Kluggmann winked at Lange who nodded. Together they crawled out of the shell hole.

In a minute, two distinct Lebel shots rang out followed by two more. The last volley was punctuated with a grenade explosion close to Braun's men who cleared out of their work for the safety of the strong point's deep trenches. Someone began shouting alarm as Kluggmann and Lange crawled back into the shell hole. A machine gun strafed the area sending stones hurtling over Kowalski's and Liebermann's heads. They cursed as loud as they could. There was nothing worse than getting shot from one's own machine guns. The no-name soldiers could only stare in amazement as they realized what had just happened.

"Are you Old Folks insane?" one of them shouted. "A completed communications trench means relief from this place." Kluggmann's otherwise neutral face glared menacingly and then just as quickly turned into a helpless, almost sheepish expression as he explained what Lange and he had just done.

"Ya see those bodies over there?" Kluggmann pointed to small mounds that could have been bodies. "Lange and me saw that those Frenchies were just playing at being dead so we crawled out there to save your lives. It's too bad they got off a few shots. And, that grenade! Why Lange here nearly got caught in it." Lange put the back of his hand on his brow to indicate a theatrical look of fear and relief. Then Kluggmann's face took on a menacing, dark look. His upper lip rolled back in what appeared to be an almost dog like snarl to show gnashing teeth. He drew out his bayonet and waved it around. "We snuck up on them and slit their throats."

"You're lying," said one of the no-name soldiers.

Kluggmann got close to him pushing his hard, muscular body against the no-name's chest and thrust his bayonet under his nose. "Look at the blood!" The soldier cringed. There was no doubt what Kluggmann's intentions were should the soldier protest to anyone. To add to the moment, Lange also showed his teeth in a snarl. Kowalski, who had stopped digging to watch the skit, turned away to hide his smile and control his impending laughter. Liebermann dropped his shovel and scrambled to take up a guard position. He comically put his hand to his brow like a red Indian to scrutinize the surroundings. He pantomimed a look of surprise and discovery, grasped his rifle, chambered a round and took aim. His Mauser erupted. The sound startled everyone who looked to him for an explanation. Kluggmann sheathed his bayonet and hurriedly crawled to Liebermann's side.

"I knew they would attack," he mumbled over and over. Liebermann winked at him.

"Ha! They can't fool me either! That one moved! He was going to throw a bomb but I got him before he could spark it." Kluggmann looked at him noticeably disappointed. Both of the no-name soldiers cringed even more. There had always been a rumor that the Old Folks were insane murderers who had been conscripted from the asylums for their killing abilities. These actions showed just how true the rumors might be. A French machine gun from the right spoke and more dirt and stones fell over the hole's occupants as bullets whizzed over their heads. Everyone took cover. The entertainment had become serious. The no-name soldiers whispered among themselves and resolved to escape the holes and the Old Folks at the first opportunity.

Bugles blared. Six shells exploded in quick succession in front of Liebermann's position. Lange and Kluggmann were thrown against the opposite shell hole wall by the rounds' concussions while Kowalski and Liebermann were airborne and propelled into the open area nearly ten meters away. The two no-name soldiers never moved but their eyes glazed over into the cold of death.

Lange was the first to recover. His hearing was gone but he could see. Kluggmann lay sprawled next to him still clutching his rifle. He crawled to him and hit him flatly in the chest.

"Kluggmann, wake up!" It was strange not hearing the sound of his own voice despite the fact that he had said something. He wondered if he had indeed said something or merely thought it and never vocalized it. He made a concerted effort to get words out of his mouth shouting again, "Come on you old sod. Wake up!" Lange questioned if it was any good to shout. After all, if his hearing was gone, Kluggmann's hearing was probably gone too. Pantomime, he thought. He began to think. The enemy will be coming now. Those shells were to neutralize this end of the line where the gap was and there was clear evidence that the trench was being extended. Lange shouted at himself mentally, 'They mustn't break through'. He looked for support to the no-name soldiers. They sat facing him with eyes wide open. He began acting out what they should do but they didn't respond. They sat next to one another staring ahead with mouths wide open as if they were surprised. Then Lange noticed the small trickle of blood that ran down their necks from their ears. A more searching look revealed that shell splinters had pierced their helmets in many places. Undoubtedly their brains were mush.

Kluggmann's hand grabbed Lange's shoulder. Lange's heart leaped into his mouth. It was as if the dead had come back to life. Kluggmann's mouth was open but Lange couldn't hear a word. Lange pointed to his ears and shook his head. Kluggmann understood and made the same motions. Two deaf soldiers stared at one another in an effort to surmise what they should do next and how to indicate those ideas to one another. Kluggmann saw that the no-name soldiers were dead. To Lange he asked about Kowalski and Liebermann by pointing to where the two had been. Lange shrugged. Then he checked his rifle and signed that Lange should do the same. Lange's rifle was missing. He picked up the dead one's rifle and opened the breach. For some reason he felt happy and relieved that it was loaded. He closed the breach chambering the first round and looked at Kluggmann still smiling. Kluggmann smiled back; it was a fiendishly satisfying smile. The two of them poked their heads over the shell crater's rim and slowly eased the rifles' muzzles over it. Lange's hearing was beginning to return. It was like being at the bottom of a pool of water. Sounds came to him but they were as if someone was calling from a distance. The constant artillery shell explosions were muted to a crump sound that very much reminded him of a heart beat. Kluggmann pointed to two grey uniformed shapes in the distance. One lay still while the other was flopping back and forth as if it were a scrap of cloth nailed to a board in a strong wind. The still form became more animated. An appendage resembling an arm appeared on the form. It reached over and clouted the scrap of material that fluttered in the wind. The scrap moved no more. Then the form rolled over and sprouted four legs or hands and legs on which it stood. Something like a head appeared and moved from side to side. Lange was reminded of an animal that had just awakened from deep sleep. Clearly, the animal was a human trying to determine where it was. Lange shouted to the shape. Then he reminded himself of the hearing loss and that the form may also be suffering from such a loss. The once convulsing scrap of material had also become a human and also crouched low on hands and knees. Kluggmann waved his arm trying to get their attention. The two forms saw the wave. The scrap and the form rose and ran toward Lange and Kluggmann. A machine gun spoke but the bullets lost the race or it was sighted too high to do any injury. The scrap and the form threw themselves to the shell hole's floor. Liebermann and Kowalski lived. Their ordeal was one to tell grandchildren about around the fireplace in the waning years of life. Either one of the soldiers could explain to their offspring how artillery explosions had heaved them high into the air propelling them over many meters to land safe and sound while others died. They had been like Baron Munchhausen in his escapades with the Turkish artillery before Vienna. They would explain to the children who sat in front of them with their mouths open and popping eyeballs how they had not been scratched while two others had had their brains liquefied.

Kluggman said nothing but motioned that they should take up positions on opposite sides to the hole, Lange and Kluggmann on one side and Liebermann and Kowalski on the other. It was as if they were in the age old defensive posture, backs to one another facing outward toward any direction from which the enemy could come. All four of them still gasped for breath but the loss of hearing soothed their nerves. The lack of noise gave them a feeling of security. Their senses involuntarily relaxed releasing pressure from the mind that had listened to days of constant crashing. Deafness became an opiate. Kowalski wanted to bathe himself in the silence. His muscles untensed as if he was in a warm bath. His eyes drooped and sleep overtook what should have been an alert conscience. His head began to fall forward nudging Liebermann's shoulder. Liebermann slapped him awake and pointed to the blue shapes approaching. Kowalski saw three rocklike objects hurling toward him. In a split second he knew they were bombs. He put his head down trusting to his steel helmet to absorb the shock and any shrapnel that came his way. At the same time he pulled Liebermann's, whose attention had been diverted in waking him, sleeve down. Liebermann looked down to where he felt the pull just as the grenades exploded. The action of looking down had caused his helmet to take the flying stones and dust that the grenade explosions kicked up while his face had avoided any flying debris. They caught their breath and raised their faces in time to see the blue uniforms. Two men carrying very large knives were only seven meters away. They were the dreaded Senegalese. Kowalski wanted to wet his pants and run. He had heard that the Senegalese were blood thirsty warriors who ate the flesh of those they wounded or killed. His trigger finger jerked and his Mauser loosed a bullet. One of the men fell. Liebermann shot the other one. Kowalski congratulated himself. He felt that he had overcome his fears in the blinking of an eye. He chambered another round. Let the black men come he shouted in triumph to himself. He had bested the first black man he had ever seen. 'They may be fierce fighters,' he told himself, 'even horrific, but they were not immune to German bullets.' They could be killed, he reasoned.

Kluggmann took aim and squeezed off a shot to see a revolver carrying blue uniform go tumbling backwards into the man that was closest to him. Lange was throwing grenades with deadly accuracy. The silence of his temporary deafness made him daring or foolish. Instead of simply tossing grenades non-stop, he would throw one and then look to see if and where it detonated. That looking after the grenade came from his not being able to hear and not in an effort to be more proficient. The looking dispelled the fear of whether or not he was fusing the grenades properly. Because he looked, he could see an effect and specific targets to throw at. It was a wonder that he wasn't shot as he dumbly stuck his head over the hole's rim to look at the explosions. Each of Kluggmann's shots toppled one enemy after another. He counted the rounds to keep from running out. He didn't want to make an error. To him, there was nothing more embarrassing then pulling the trigger on a spent cartridge or an empty chamber. After five shots he left the breach open, fumbled in his ammunition pouch, and pulled out a stripper clip filled with another five rounds. The clip fitted neatly into the rifle chamber and with a thumb he pushed the bullets into the magazine, closed the breach on the first round and began firing again. The whole action took only seconds although it felt as if hours passed.

Kluggmann had lost touch with his charges. 'Were they all right?' he asked himself. He interrupted his shooting to look around. He saw that Lange had run out of grenades and had begun shooting at the attacking figures. The no-name soldiers sat smiling at them as if they were delighted about something which had escaped Kluggmann's observation. He regretted threatening those two even if it was in jest. He made a mental note to justify his behavior toward them later to either Kowalski or Lange. They would understand. Kowalski would probably explain the whole incident away as he always did. His eyes fell on Liebermann who was crawling around collecting ammunition from the dead. Liebermann tapped each of the soldiers' boots as he put a punch of cartridges at their feet. Next to Lange he placed more grenades. Lange hurriedly put his rifle aside and recommenced throwing the grenades. Machine gun bullets like angry insects began arcing over their hole and into the enemy. Braun was adding his support to Kluggmann's position. The blue uniforms fell in tens. The French faltered, stopped their forward motion and began returning to the safety of their former trenches. The momentum of the attack was broken. A few tried to run for the Old Folks' hole to seek shelter. Kluggmann shot two but others took cover and threw grenades. Strangely enough the grenades landed in the newly dug crawl trench instead of the occupied shell hole. The shallow trench seemed to be a decoy. The Senegalese had thought it was the main trench because of the newly dug dirt piled in front of it. Lange countered the bomb attack with three quickly thrown stick bombs. The attackers did not move from their cover. Kluggmann called a cease fire only to have his order punctuated with an increase in artillery shells. The air became toxic. Kowalski yelled gas and waved his hands about to show that he was getting his mask on. Masks covered the faces of all in seconds and an eerie fog covered the Old Folks who lay back gasping within their masks.

Chapter 4
Interlude

18/V/16

Dearest One,

    If you are reading this letter than you know that these are my last words. I hope that one of my good friends, Kluggmann, Liebermann, or Kowalski has delivered it to your hands. I do not expect it to reach you in any promptness since soldiers are not post-men who have established routes or even an obligation to deliver the correspondence left in their hands. It is quite probable that this will not reach you until the end of the war. Please give a few marks to the person who delivers it.

    Hopefully, the deliverer will tell you how I met my end. If this is delivered by someone else who was not there, believe me when I say that there is no pain at the end. I have had many describe it to me as a release of all pain although they have not experienced it themselves. I will remain a skeptic until the end. I'm sorry for such a bad joke at such a sad time. I only do it to keep you from sad thoughts.

    There was so much that I wanted to tell you before you received this letter but now it is too late. Can I say that I missed the warmth of your lap and the soothing words you said to me as a child to make me fall asleep after a terrible nightmare? I kept those words close to my heart always and said them to myself many times during this war. Even among the shell bursts, those few syllables calmed me. But let me tell you where you may find me should you come looking for me after the war.

I will be among the mud and bricks of Verdun. I'm sorry I can't be more specific for a soldier's grave in this war is one of opportune space. We have no time for formal funerals or for digging the right size hole and bundling up a body in a coffin. That is for renowned officers and, as we well know, I am not one of that breed. Don't feel appalled at this but most of us are wrapped in a water proof sheet and placed in a hole with sixty or seventy others. Sometimes we are buried on the spot where we fell with only a rifle stuck in the ground over us as a marker. In either case, it makes no difference to me. I cannot protest nor should you since tens of thousands have received similar treatment and they were probably more of a hero than I.

Please tell Elsa that I was very fond of her and would have begun courting her had I returned. I always felt that we were more than just good friends. She is so much like you. I never told her of my feelings nor did I even think she noticed the small things I did for her. I was willing to make a try though. I'm sure she will feel no remorse over my death. The admiration is probably only with me and I joke with myself that she did in fact know of my existence.

But let me tell you of the fine fellows I have been serving with this last year. First, there's Kluggmann, a finer soldier there never was. But that's all he knows. He had been retired shortly before the war began and allotted the government position of mail handler. In his own words, he had almost gone to seed. The war had revived his warrior spirit but I fear that he will not survive the war for if he does he will not be of any use anywhere unless it is in a job of killing. If he brings you the letter, tell him I looked up to him as a teacher in survival. Without him, this letter would have arrived much sooner. Second is Liebermann, a man of the cosmopolitan Berlin streets. He is a charmer with all the ladies. If he delivers the letter don't let him near the silver. Finally, there is Kowalski the scholar. Be prepared for a long dissertation about the futility of war and the purpose of the soldier in history if he brings this letter. He has a reason for everything that has happened probably including my death.

I know you will be shocked that I have fallen in with these sorts but we seem to compliment one another. Imagine, we four came from different positions and we would have never met if it hadn't been for this war. We took care of one another in the most dangerous of times and laughed in the most relaxed. They were true comrades.

Let me talk about the more practical and less romantic side of soldiering. Remember you are entitled to a soldier's pension. It won't be much but at least it will buy food for the table. Go to the regimental headquarters and they will give you the forms to fill out. Remember my number and rank.

There was so much more I would have liked to have said in this final letter but we don't want it to be a burden to the carrier. If our pastor is correct, we will meet again and it will be like there is no time between meetings. Then we can talk for an eternity.

With all my love,

Peter

Chapter 5
1200 – 1500

Braun's half company had gone to the trenches unprepared. The water that the men had carried in their flasks had run out quickly as did the supply of hand grenades. The continued probing French patrols had exhausted the meager supply of grenades, two per soldier, while the men, new to the trenches and unaware how quickly fear dries the mouth, had over indulged in drinking their water. It wasn't long before Braun decided that someone had to go to the rear to bring up supplies. Being the egalitarian and wanting to test his popularity, Braun had asked for volunteers to fetch the needed provisions but none had stepped forward. In desperation he had cajoled and tried to joke his way into getting someone to volunteer but his nicety had failed. Brow beating them with guilt did not work either. He became discouraged. Until that moment he thought of himself as being popular and often bragged to Pfeiffer that his men idolized him and would not hesitate in following him into hell. How sorely disappointed he was.

'How I have lavished favors on you,' Braun said to himself as he searched the dirty, mud caked faces of his men for some sign of loyalty. 'I made sure that your duties were light in rest areas and got you passes to the brothels.' It was apparent to him that his efforts had come to nothing. As his head sagged forward in surrender to the human spirit the answer to his dilemma crossed his mind in a lightning flash. 'Of course! Leadership had nothing to do with popularity!' In an instant he realized that command required the leader to make decisions without regard to popularity or in garnering respect. As an after thought, he saw his previous life flash before him. Everything had been so much easier as a corps supply sergeant but war had presented opportunities that he could not have passed up. The deaths of many of the prewar line noncommissioned officers had garnered for him promotion without having to show an aptitude for leadership. And the multitude of deaths among the professional officers who had ruled over company commands since the 1870 war allowed for lower ranks to achieve the pinnacle of leadership: command, of course, under officer supervision. However, attrition was a two edged sword. His supply duties were shifted to a Landstrum man who was too feeble for an active role in the trenches and , with his new rank, he soon found himself in the field and in vice command of an infantry company. The men of two platoons called him sir, doffed their hats, and talked about him behind his back.

At first Braun was frightened about going to the front. What did a life of leading men have in store for him he had puzzled to himself during the long train ride to France to join the companies? By the time he arrived in the line he had resigned himself to the task and reasoned out that men would follow him if he made them comfortable. He had taken on the persona of a doting uncle joking with the men and petting their heads. With his connections in regimental supply channels, he had made sure the men wanted for neither rations nor equipment. However, after this volunteer incident he saw how ungrateful and selfish men faced with their own death could be.

Braun shook his head like a dog who was attempting to shake off a fly that buzzed his nose on a hot summer day. The motion rearranged his thoughts and from it he drew a new sense of purpose.

Braun decided on the one course that was open to him and would hopefully garner him the respect that he thought he had already captured. He selected two men purposely and with authority, calling them by their surnames and pointing at them as a father would point to his offspring to indicate displeasure. In his eyes the men had become cows, cows that needed to be prodded into the slaughterhouse. Despairingly the two selectees lowered their heads and stepped forward toward the slaughterhouse door. They smelled the blood from within and realized that they too were for the slaughter. Braun did not smile. He looked earnestly at their downturned heads. Inside his slow mind he shouted: 'see what you have forced me to do'. Outwardly, he became benevolent. With a smile he said with authority deeply embedded in his voice, "I want you to go to the right and relieve the Old Folks," he told the two selectees. "Tell them to report to me." The two trotted off. Once again they were frolicking calves in a field of new clover. They chided one another with pulled punches. They had cheated death for the time being. Braun made a mental note of who those people were so he could hold this over their heads as an obligation when he had no other options. 'That is how respect and loyalty are garnered from soft men,' he thought below the smirk that had involuntarily crossed his face. 'It was through threats and debts.' That was a game he had become a master of before the war.

Kluggmann's group soon appeared. Braun stood with his legs slightly apart and his hands on his hips. He cautioned himself not to straighten up too far and give the sniper a target. His face scowled, his mouth fairly sneered. In a deep voice, with a tone which negated any argument he said, "I need two of you to volunteer to get water and hand grenades from the rear." Braun congratulated himself on keeping his voice firm and level but a searching glance of the Old Folks' faces showed that the new Braun did not impress either Kluggmann or Kowalski. Old soldiers are used to harsh tones while conscripts have an engrained trait that makes them scoff at authority. Neither of them would volunteer themselves. Liebermann and Lange were of a different cut. One had lived his entire life as a member of the oppressed poor on which authority preyed. He had learned to survive through cooperation and manipulation. The other was a volunteer imbued with a desire to please authority. Without a word, each entrusted their rifles and packs to their two comrades, nodded to Braun and started down the communications trench. Kowalski's prediction had come true. With the shell holes connected to the company strong point, Braun had asserted his authority over them. It didn't matter that they were just on loan and already exhausted. As his two comrades turned to their task, Kowalski could plainly see that the Old Folks would be the brunt of every indelicate work detail until relieved simply because Braun wanted to maintain his popularity with his own men even at the cost of others' lives.

The communication trench was treacherous but it was safe. Its two and a half meter high walls were slimy and the floor, because of the high water table in the area, was unstable even in the driest conditions. The pioneers had lined the trench floor with duckboards that were supposed to make treading safe; however, there were many places where the boards shifted at the slightest pressure or floated in a pool of molten earth. There were other places where the duckboards were firm even though the water stood knee deep above them. Liebermann and Lange had traveled the route many times and both of them had a personal fear to overcome each time they walked on the boards. Lange feared disorientation. One wrong turn could put a soldier into the enemy occupied areas where the humiliation of capture would await or into an artillery or machine gun kill zone where death would greet them. Liebermann's fear was more sinister. He had traveled along the duckboards often enough not to get lost even though the constant shelling and heavy rains often destroyed landmarks. Each time he made the trip he trusted to instinct rather than landmarks. He was like a sea captain measuring the number of paces in one direction and shifting to another direction on completion of a specified duration. Then he was back to counting paces again in preparation for the next deviation. The protection of the trench depth allowed him to concentrate on the number of paces. Liebermann's fear was beneath his paces and at his shoulder. It was the mud.

Liebermann took the lead setting a loping pace like that of a horse at a parade. Lange broke into the prescribed regulation trot but soon realized that Liebermann's pace was not too uniform nor was it faster than the proscribed pace. It was quick where the duckboards were firmer but slowed where they slipped from side to side. The pace not only compensated for the terrain it also gave way to the traffic from other units that shared the communication trench. The traffic consisted of messengers, stretcher bearers with or without loads, walking wounded and supply details like themselves. Liebermann dodged around the human obstacles like an experienced city cab driver whose fare had given him instructions to make haste at the busiest time of day. One thing he could not compensate his pace for were the clogs caused by the stretcher bearers with their loads of wounded, moaning men. Sometimes two carried a litter and other times there were four. It didn't matter how many there were, rather, it was the fact that they walked in the dead center of the trench forcing everyone to plaster themselves up against the trench walls until the stretcher had passed. Sometimes they stopped to check bandages or administer water to the carried one which either stopped traffic entirely or forced the passers-by to leap over the carriers and stretcher. Liebermann cursed all those who were slower or those who were going in the opposite direction. When they came upon stretcher bearers, he confided to Lange that they should throw the poor blighter out of the trench since the doctors would probably kill the man on the operating table anyway. But after the words were spoken, Liebermann would lower his head and apologize for what he had said. He knew that he could be that man on the stretcher at any moment and he would want someone to make an effort to save his life.

Normally, the communication trench would be deserted at this time of day. Rations details and the evacuation of wounded were normally done in the evening when darkness hid movements but that day was ideal. The sky had become overcast after the morning's sunshine filled clearness and it was beginning to show a promise of rain. The clouds were low. As a result, the bloated observation balloons and vulture like aeroplanes, of which the enemy had many, were not aloft. Such an opportunity for movement in daylight had led to an exodus of men from the front to the rear. They found comfort in the gray of their uniforms and the grayness of the clouds and mud. The two hues blended so well that a moving man was almost rendered invisible to any ground observer.

Lange was keeping up. Liebermann was happy for that. Those who had accompanied him on other ration parties had tried to take charge. Liebermann had let them and the result was always the same. The party became lost or the leader was wounded or killed. In the end, it was he who took charge and got the job done. Too often, he took charge only after all had wandered off or been killed. 'That was their bad luck,' Liebermann thought to himself. 'Many would still be alive if only they had listened to my silence.' He stopped when he reached a corner around which the trench would continue. Protruding from the wall were the roots of an ancient tree. It was a tangled mess of hundreds of taproots with diameters of a few centimeters wrapped around main roots that had the thickness of a man's thigh or upper arm. Once, the roots had supported a mighty oaken stem that had weathered drought and floods for years or probably centuries but the constant artillery barrages were too much for the branches. The boughs had disintegrated leaving only a thick jaggedly cut stump and the roots. Yet the tree would not go softly. Its broken off trunk shaped into the image of an upraised fisted arm seemed to scream defiance at any more shells.

"We can get a breather here," he said turning to Lange whose face clearly showed relief. "No one can see you here, not even the flying machines or sausages when they are up. Remember this spot. See here how the roots are dried white? At night, these old roots actually glow. You can see them clearly from a distance." Lange nodded. "This is your sign to take the right communicator to get back to the company or the left to get to the supply areas. That other trench leads to nowhere safe. Stay out of it. I tell you these things to make sure you can get back without me. We have only about six more meters to go before we come out of the trench and into open ground then we should be able to see the company strongpoint just another fifty meters away among fallen trees. You remember?" Lange nodded. "The rest of the company is there hidden among the fallen trees. Deep underground. But don't think for a second that we are safe this far back from the firing line. That open country between the end of the communicator and the strongpoint is where the French are dropping shells, big ones, and where Braun's men got machine gunned. When we get to the open area it's each to his own. Don't worry about me and I won't worry about you. We will have to cross that area as best we can. Stay low when we run across it and don't straighten up until we reach the forest. Take advantage of any cover you see if the shooting gets heavy. I'll do the same. I'm not trying to be over cautious. You're my comrade but I can't watch out for you when I'm trying to make sure I survive. Do you understand?" Lange nodded again. He knew that comradeship had nothing to do with survival. If Liebermann were to catch a packet, Lange would not stop to help. This wasn't the first time Lange had been on ration detail although Liebermann treated him that way. He didn't mind. Liebermann was an expert at it. He always returned with the goods he was sent for while others did not. There was no need for words or questions. He trusted Liebermann who smiled and patted him on the shoulder. "Let's go." He took off in the fast lope that Lange had been copying.

They had been blessed so far in their journey. Liebermann attributed it to the low clouds which kept the aeroplanes from flying and the balloons down. Besides, the French were probably dozing or finishing one of the gourmet meals they were reputed to have over there according to the leaflets that were dropped over German trenches imploring the soldiers to give themselves up. Relaxation. A full belly. These vices were always in Liebermann's thoughts. But in order to get those precious things, a person had to be alive. He thought many times about sneaking out one night to give himself up but there was guarantee that he would be welcome with open arms. Too many French soldiers hated the Germans so much that they would shoot first rather than allow surrender. The thought of a soft life as a prisoner flitted away. There was a more important matter on Liebermann's mind and that was on forming a plan by which he and Lange would carry thirty liters of water and a crate of grenades back the way they had come. He reasoned that he would need a pole. On that shaft he would suspend the load. He and Lange would shoulder each end of the pole with the supplies in the middle. They would be like the Swiss milkmaids who carried milk from their barns to the processing house. Liebermann thought, 'If those rosy cheeked damsels could shoulder what must have been heavy loads, just think how much two virile lads could handle.'

Soon they reached the end of the communication trench and faced the open ground. Liebermann crouched down to survey the territory. It never really changed. Liebermann was just being thorough. It was a jumbled mess of shallow almost connected shell holes that afforded no cover. Some of the craters were filled with putrid water in which corpses floated while others were no deeper than half a meter. There was no cover. In olden times, at least before the war, the area had been a clearing in the middle of the forest. Locals had probably made up stories to explain why trees didn't grow there. Witches danced there on Sabbath nights or maybe it was cursed or a death of supernatural origins had occurred there. The old tales mattered little. Now it was a killing field of not more than sixty meters square into which the French poured shrapnel or machine gun bullets. Liebermann's diminutive balk at the end of the narrow communicator acted as a plug to the human flow. Those behind him called out that he should go on but Liebermann did not move. Instead, he motioned to them to pass him. A few pushed him aside but went no further than a meter. Light artillery shells fused to explode three meters above the ground strewed the beaten space with shrapnel balls. The deadly balls came as a torrent of rain; a metal rain of drops that were five or six centimeters in circumference. They plowed up the turf sending puffs of earth in all directions. Lange guessed that a ball could burrow into a human body to cripple or kill as easily as a hot knife could hole cheese. A steel helmet would offer no protection to a runner who might try to cross the distance.

"Have they seen us then?" Lange asked Liebermann who shook his head.

"Harassment fire," Liebermann responded. "I'm sure they know that this is where the main communication trench comes out in front of the strongpoint. They send over enough planes whose observers take thousands of photographs which would show a constant stream of people across this point."

"Then why don't they just destroy the position?"

"They've probably reasoned that whatever is hidden among the fallen trees is better left alone. They use it as bait; it's a gigantic mouse trap in which humans are caught. French officers have figured that we have to get into those trees and by setting down a perpetual bombardment, either cannon or machine gun, on this area they can score a few random hits. It shows you how much they have to waste if they're willing to send over so many rounds to get only a few. I'm telling you that's an indication of who's going to win the war if it comes to material." Liebermann watched for a firing pattern. He ignored the shouts from the rear that called on him to get on with it. Soon he realized that the shells exploded in groups of fours. The shooting was slow, timed and in salvos of all guns of the battery firing at one time. At that pace, there was a gap of about twenty seconds between each salvo as the guns reloaded to fire en masse again. "Right! There's about twenty to thirty seconds between the four explosions. After the next four shells, we run!" Lange nodded and turned to those who were behind and told them about the pattern. The word was passed along.

Four shells detonated strewing shrapnel bullets across the open area. Since the shells exploded at the same time, the balls all crashed to the ground at the same time. The noise was deafening and reminded Lange of a load of coal landing in the basement storage bin. Lange and Lieberman stood up and ran. They both kept their bodies erect to increase their speed. A crouching run would have only slowed them and afforded no protection against death from above. Despite having told Lange that it was each man for himself, Liebermann ran alongside him coaxing him on. "No stopping for breath! Move!" There was a pant filled interlude of silence and then a shout. "Down!" Lange flopped to the ground. The next four shells came crashing in. A bloody screaming soldier fell across Lange. Lange looked at the dead face expecting to see Liebermann's brown eyes but instead he saw the face of a stranger. Some of the men behind them had followed them out. Too many. A few of the bullets had bounced off Lange's helmet but the majority of the shot shredded the man who lay across him. The smoke cleared in a few moments and the shrapnel bullets ceased falling. Lange, powered by fear, used his feet and hands to push the corpse off him and then he was running again. In seconds, he was among the fallen trees where he was met with cheers and a firm handshake from Liebermann and the rest of the company. The company had watched the foot race with rapt attention from the safety of positions dug under the trees' corpses. Older soldiers had bet the younger replacements on whether the two would make the safety of the underbrush alive. Naturally, the replacements had no knowledge of the Old Folk's phenomenal survival rate. Many cigarettes, the common currency for wagers, changed hands. Lange took one look back to see how the traffic was faring. It came in small groups at regular intervals. He felt a remorse for the stretcher bearers who weren't as fast as individual runners.

Pfeiffer appeared having heard the commotion in his shelter. He caught Lange in a quizzical look. "What news from the forward point. Have the French broken through? Are you two all that is left?" Pfeiffer was unable to keep emotion out of his questions. He could hide his facial emotions but without purposeful restraint, eagerness dripped from his words. And there was good cause for the anxiousness. If the position was lost, he would have only a few minutes to plan and launch a counterattack. Battalion would expect him to take the initiative. If he did not, he would be relieved.

"I beg to report that Vizefeldwebel Braun sent Grenadiers Liebermann and Lange to get water and hand grenades," Lange said standing at attention. "The enemy was silent when we left and the position was secure. We had repulsed a new attack a little earlier with not casualties." Pfeiffer calmed himself. More good news. The fact that half his company not directly under his supervision had beat back an attack with no casualties would have to come to the attention of the higher ups and garner him some type of recognition. His next report would make special mention of how his training had lowered casualty rates since his arrival. In the meantime he took special note of Lange's posture.

'Here's a good soldier,' Pfeiffer thought. 'Well educated for a young man. This is a man destined to be a builder of the future.'

Despite treating Lange in such a gruff manner and distancing himself from a more congenial attitude, he liked him. It was part of his demeanor to treat everyone with disgust outwardly while taking an affectionate tone internally. As a former factory supervisor he was good at recognizing leadership potential. When he had taken command he had been initially attracted to Kowalski, a man who reasoned his existence but Pfeiffer's interest had soon waned as the philosopher showed a streak of romanticism tempered by questionable logic and definite socialist tendencies. But in Lange, Pfeiffer saw an untapped enthusiasm about things that were happening. He saw that Lange was not solely concerned about survival. Lange could see a much larger picture of the war than most. Pfeiffer had gone so far as to approach leadership subjects with Lange by posing tactical problems. Lange had not been afraid to respond honestly coming up with solutions that Pfeiffer agreed with or presenting a side that he had not anticipated. Pfeiffer had thought of transferring Lange to another squad but, because of his reputation with the Old Folks, no one wanted him. Perhaps in a few months, if he and Lange survived, he could recommend him for officer training. He admired Lange's respectful stance for a few more moments before answering.

"At ease, Lange, you don't want to get me shot do you?" Lange relaxed his stance and thought the lieutenant was over cautious. His attitude toward Pfeiffer had been influenced by Kluggmann. Many moments had passed since he had come to attention in front of the officer. If a sharpshooter had seen him stand to attention in front of this man only seconds would have elapsed before a shot would have ended Pfeiffer's life. "Water is over there, you know, and the grenades are at the dump under those fallen trees. Have the French given up on their assaults yet?"

"I wish to report that they are sending out single or two man patrols to find weak spots," responded Liebermann who came to attention ignoring the warning Pfeiffer had given Lange. The lieutenant flashed a dagger glare at Liebermann who relaxed his stance. He looked at the scrawny man with the gaze that was all too obvious and spoke volumes of disgust.

'The Jew. Such a wonderful asset to the company but a Jew nevertheless.' Pfeiffer thought. 'He's been infected by Kluggmann. Too many old soldier habits. I must see that he will be volunteering for dangerous missions whenever possible in the future.'

Liebermann ignored the cold stare and went on. "We have connected the line out to the right flank. There are still a few meters that are open between us and the Bavarians but we have an arrangement with the Bavarians to cover the area in crossfire."

"Ah, so. Braun is such a capable person. Arrange that, did he?" Pfeiffer asked. Lange refrained from blurting out that he had done the arranging while Braun had sat in his dugout doing something of no importance. He held his comments because he had seen what happened to resourceful men in the army. Special recognition often led to promotion and added responsibilities. He wanted none of it. He simply nodded. "When do you think Braun will release your section back to me?"

"I am not sure of his intentions, Herr Lieutenant." Lange began to snap to attention before leaving but relaxed when distress showed in Pfeiffer's expression. He asked for permission to seek the supplies he had been sent for and the lieutenant nodded. Liebermann and he turned and disappeared in the direction of water and the grenade depot; Lange for the grenades and Liebermann for the water. They would meet with their loads at the point where they had entered the strong point.

The harvesting took only a few minutes and each was back at the entrance that led to the communications trench. Liebermann arrived first to survey the open area. He thanked his lucky stars that the overcast sky had begun shedding rain. Nature's tears would give them more cover than just an overcast sky could; however, the trenches would become mud baths. The trench walls had not been lined as a safety measure. Higher authority had reasoned after a careful review of the causes of casualties that revetment boards became deadly projectiles when hit with high explosive shells. Therefore, lining the trenches was strictly forbidden. As a result, when it rained, trenches sometimes disappeared. The tops simply oozed away to the bottom of the trench where they merged with the mire that existed there. The walls of three meter deep trenches had often leveled themselves in minutes taking away the protection and the direction markers. Where companies had defied the order to shore up the trench sides, things were not better. There the water accumulated to depths of a meter or two. Duckboards floated like so many toy boats at city parks' ponds on a summer's day. In either case revetments or not, the trenches became seas of liquid earth. The oozing, sticky, grasping mud, Liebermann's bête noire, could suck a man into its depths in an instant to drown him as friends stood by helplessly watching. Taking to the ground around the trenches was equally dangerous not only because of the snipers that hunted the area looking for just such targets but also because the flat shell pock marked ground was just as unstable as that in the trench.

Liebermann had found a stout branch that they could use as a carrying pole for the water and hand grenades. Always an opportunist, he hung the grenade box toward the end he would be carrying and the water near Lange. He had rightly surmised that the grenades would be lighter than the water justifying the load positioning by saying that Lange was fitter than he. Of course, convenience had its draw backs. The carrying method meant that they would have to stay together in order to make it back. Individual initiative which was so necessary in self preservation when shells began to fall or machine guns laid a barrage was negated. Liebermann could never hope to get such a load back by himself. He needed Lange. As a result, the two may have well been handcuffed together.

Bets were already being made with a ten to one ratio against Liebermann and Lange making it across open ground with such a load suspended between them. Liebermann had already noted a pattern to the enemy's fire over the open area. While they had gathered the cargo and rested, the enemy had changed from artillery to machine gun fire over the clearing. Clods of earth were exploding across the expanse and the air was filled with multiple bullets. Lange pointed out that the cone of fire was around the approach to the wood. Its depth was only a few meters and there was only one gun firing. All they had to do was cross those few meters and they would be safe for the rest of the trip to the communication trench. Their time to move would come when the machine gun interrupted its fire to keep the barrel from overheating. They watched for an interval and it came in a few minutes. Replenishing the gun's water jacket would take a few minutes. They ran almost doubled in two hoping that the enemy wouldn't simply pass the work off to a new gun that would open fire immediately. Those who remained behind cheered. After a few paces, they were outside of the cone of fire and safe to slow their pace. They reached the communication trench almost standing upright. Liebermann's opinion of Vizefeldwebel Braun sank lower as he realized Braun had needlessly sacrificed his men to the barrage, probably to meet a timetable. As they trotted off along the communication trench, the rainfall took on its own pace, not driving but steady. There was no avoiding the huge drops. They thumped mercilessly on their helmets and got into their eyes and mouth. The drink was refreshing but it often choked Lange who was breathing in pants again.

The communication trench was only a meter and a half wide at its broadest expanse. Liebermann and Lange had suspended the water container and the box of grenades on a long branch between them. They should have walked side by side but the trench walls would not allow it. Instead they walked single file with Liebermann leading. The weight of the articles did not allow him to break into his steady loping pace nor a quick one. The team had to maintain a beeline approach rather than a route that could zig and zag through the crowd that they were going against. There was also the instability of the quickly flooding trench floor. Liebermann had developed a pace in response to these obstacles but more so because of the unstable floor. His gait never allowed his entire weight to bear down on the duckboards and as a result he never became a victim of the mud that lay like a wolf below the boards. He involuntarily shuttered. One year's war had hardened Liebermann against the most nauseating sights. He had played practical jokes with corpses and putrid body parts but the muck and the mire that dwelled below his feet were constant sources of nightmares. There had been many times that he had watched as a soldier who stood too long on one board slowly sank into the mud with the board beneath his feet. It was as if the earth opened a mouth at the unwary soldier's feet and slowly sucked him into its dirt lined stomach. Sometimes the extraction of one man took as many as six men. Sometimes there was nothing anyone could do and the soldier soon disappeared into a murky depth. The most horrifying sight Liebermann had ever seen was when dryness shrank the mud and revealed the shriveled corpses of those who had not had aid when they had become prey to the mud wolves. Their deaths must have been terrifying, Liebermann had thought. They had drowned and suffocated at the same time. How long had it taken for death to come to those in such a predicament? Did they scream for help to the very last breath?

To Liebermann the muck was a vicious wolf with a mouth lined with gripping teeth that sucked a man backwards into its stomach. He had wakened himself from many dreams in which the beast had taken him into its mouth. Slowly the tongue and jaws had taken him deeper and deeper. He had tried to claw at the mouth's sides which only oozed over his fingers and slipped up his sleeves. There was no escape. This trip was how his dream began. He was frightened to the point of gasping for air. He loathed the fact that the pace that was required to keep the load balanced and Lange following closely was not as light and quick as he would have wished. There were steps where he felt the boards shift under his weight and that of the load. He was sure that the mud wolves were already dogging his every step wishing that he would misstep and then they would snap him in. He put his hand out to the walls to steady himself but quickly pulled it back as the mud oozed over his fingers. The walls were part of the wolves. He felt afraid and hesitated in putting his foot down. The pace was broken. The momentary pause caused the box of grenades to hit him in the back. Lange had not been warned of the lapse in stride and had kept the pace.

"Hey, give me some warning when you're going to stop," Lange said in a peeved tone as the water container recoiled and thudded against his chest. After thirty-six hours without sleep Lange was no longer the amicable gymnasium student. Liebermann grunted and picked up the pace. Lange regretted making the comment as he tried to keep up. The boards quaked under his feet also. He also knew of the danger that would grasp his boot if he even lightly touched the mud. They rounded a corner and were confronted by stretcher bearers carrying two wounded men. The rule was to give way to the wounded by sidling over to one side. In a trench that was only a meter or two wide both groups had to be acrobats to maintain their footing on the boards. Lange and Liebermann leaned to the right plunging their shoulders into the semi-molten trench wall. Some of the trench wall oozed down the sleeves of their blouses that were upturned because of the way they steadied the pole between them. The stretcher bearers hefted their cargos to shoulder height and never broke their stride. A bloody hand fell from beneath the blanket of the second stretcher to brush across Lange's upper arm. Could that be an omen, he asked himself?

In a minute the way was clear and Liebermann tried to get into a faster pace. But the openness was momentary. The opposing traffic in the trench grew. Walking wounded accompanied by well wishers were appearing in ever increasing numbers. When Liebermann and Lange had gone out, they had blended with this traffic. Going in to the strongpoint had been less difficult because they could merge with the traffic and they had no load to carry. In moving back to the front lines they found that the people who opposed them were as stiff as tide driven sea waves. In their supposed pain or the urgency of their mission, the walking wounded refused to give way or even to walk to one side in order to share the duckboards.

"Thick headed Prussians!" Liebermann said under his breath as he stopped and the box of grenades bounced against his back again. An idea came to him. Loudly he proclaimed, "High explosives going to the front. One side so we can avoid blowing up the whole trench if one of those shells hits us. High explosives coming through. Give us some room." The oncoming traffic froze and then like the Red Sea under Moses' direction, it leaned to one side causing a great open parting. Liebermann picked up the pace and thanked people with a smirk as he passed them. He kept shouting, "High explosives coming through. Look out. Move over. Don't delay us." Too late those who stood aside saw that the high explosives were only grenades. The curses that were hurled at their backs rolled off their coats like the rain. Then it happened.

Ahead of them, at a juncture with other communicators, they saw four men standing around another man in the middle of the trench. The middle man was slowly sinking as his comrades tried to pull him out using their rifles as ropes. The rifles were too short and slippery to be of any aid and the man's struggling only made him sink faster; pulling him out seemed to be a lost cause without a rope. He was already up to his waist. There was no getting around the plug in the trench. People began bunching up on either side of the trapped man and his comrades. Involuntarily everyone periodically looked to the sky where they expected to see incoming artillery rounds at any second. A commotion began to permeate the air. There were calls to get on, leave the man to his fate. Lange was the first to figure out a solution. He told Liebermann to let down the load. Once down, Lange withdrew the limb they had been using as a balance. He made his way into the center of the circle of men who were trying to extract their comrade and laid down the branch which easily spanned the quagmire. Lange told the soldier to place the limb in his armpits which he did. Then the five men, Liebermann stood by horrified at the sight of the sucking muck, picked up either end and lifted straight up. Slowly, the soldier's lower body reemerged until there was an audible slurp and pop and the man's feet appeared. When the soldier was free and safe on the duck boards, his comrades shook Lange's hand. The rescued man was grateful but cold since the mud had kept his boots and pants. To Liebermann, the loss of clothing proved that the mud was a hungry animal. It may have been deprived of the man's body but it feasted on his clothing as a consolation.

Lange retrieved his pole, replaced the load, and after some soldiers laid a piece of corrugated metal over the mud pit, the two were off again. The mob that had collected because of the delay gave way in their thanks for saving a comrade. The rain continued to fall as if it wanted to show the French artillery that it could put more missiles on a target than their petty cannons could ever do.

Liebermann shouted over his shoulder that the ball of roots was just up ahead. As he did he noticed that a soldier was standing by the fallen tree. A trench guard.

"Hold there," the guard commanded. Liebermann stopped and felt the weight of the grenade box once again hit him in the back. Lange swore. To keep the rain out of his eyes, Lange had had his head down. He was not only disturbed about the sudden stop but surprised by the voice.

"What's the problem?" asked Liebermann.

"Trench is blown all to hell up ahead and washed over. No protection. If you go left here you can link up with another communicator about thirty meters from here. If you're lucky that one will be intact. If not, keep going until you find one." Liebermann shook his head.

"Can't do that", he said in a voice that was both scornful and commanding. "Our company needs this stuff and they're only sixty meters to the right. We'll take our chances." The guard, not impressed by the authority in Liebermann's voice, puffed himself up to look dangerous in an effort to stop the two from going where he had said not to go. To both of the soldiers, the implied threat seemed ludicrous. The guard was a Landstrum man in his middle forties. Two months ago men like him had been brought out of Germany to do menial jobs so that fighting men could go where they were needed most. The vast majority of these Landstrum sported over sized mustaches and beards along with paunches of pudding about their waists. They looked like Father Christmas or the gingerbread men of fairy tales. No one could take such a person seriously no matter how much authority they tried to inject in their voices.

Before Liebermann could berate the guard a shell burst over their heads. The guard, deflated under the rush of hot air, cowered against the trench wall on his knees with his face down and his hands covering the back of his head. These men had not been given steel helmets since their duties rarely took them to the front lines. Liebermann and Lange stepped around him and went right. They sneered as they cleared the trench guard's quaking form. It was apparent to both of them that the brave guard was not a front hog. They had known that the shell would burst well outside of their area and posed no threat. Laying on the trench floor for such misses was a waste of time.

After five meters the trench ended in a mass of mud. Liebermann turned to Lange. Shells were exploding over the destroyed fortifications. "Rest for a bit and let's see if there's a pattern to this shooting. I need to get my bearings too. Without the trench we'll be in the open with no landmarks to guide us. I'm pretty sure the trench ran that way. I remember those two corpses to the left." He pointed at a gentle bump in the terrain that no one would have recognized as having been men. The only indication that the rise was indeed bodies was the presence of broken rifles and rusted helmets. Lange, shielding his eyes from the increased intensity of the rain with his hands, looked out over a landscape that was devoid of anything. It was simply a mass of holes. The majority of the holes was filled with water and could not be used as shelter. Neither of the two could see into the distance because of the driving rain. "Once we figure out a pattern we go in that direction. Agreed?" Liebermann pointed. Lange nodded. What argument could he offer?

The French cannons were shooting high explosives with impact fuses. The pattern was right to left and back on a line forty meters long that traversed their path. Once again it was battery fire, only four guns in use. At the least, one out of every four shells was a dud or a shell that simply buried itself in the devouring mud. Sometimes all four shells failed to detonate. Liebermann and Lange hefted their load and watched the explosions traverse the landscape to the right. The last shell detonated and the curtain moved left. A dud slammed into the ground splashing mud and water into a geyser. Liebermann grabbed his end of the tree branch, shouted something that was inaudible, and started running. Lange barely had time to pick up his end but managed to stumble after with the mire sucking at his boots. As a result of his uneven start, the two loads began swinging on the pool from side to side. The combined weights caused the runners to lurch from side to side in increasingly violent jerks. Lange wondered how long it would be before the loads simply threw the pair of them to the ground. Hours ticked by in those minutes that they ran. Where was the trench? Were they going in the right direction? Liebermann felt the teeth of the mud. He mustn't stop, he told himself, even if Lange gets it. He calculated how he would take part of the load by himself to the company and then come back with help to get the rest and either a wounded Lange or his corpse. It was then that a distant voice woke Liebermann from his calculations. He heard it as a hiss or a song. The roaring artillery bursts and sloshing mire made sounds like the crashing of waves on a rocky beach.

"Over here. Over here," the voice said in tones that carried so well. Liebermann wondered if it was Lorelei luring the two to death. Lange's ears perked up like a terrier who had heard the scratching of a rat.

Between the pants, "There's someone over there! To the right!" Lange shouted at Liebermann's ear. Liebermann nodded and shifted direction. He could not keep the rain out of his eyes. The load found the shift in direction to be stabilizing and rested; however, the swaying pace that the runners had slipped into remained the same and they ran on the sides of their feet. First right, then left. They could not stop themselves.

The voice grew louder and repeated, "Over here!" Another direction shift. Their swaying stopped and their boots slapped the face of the mud beast sending up splashes. A hand torch flashed. Liebermann's direction veered a little more and that set off the load to swaying again but the runners contained the motion. The artillery shells whistled toward them. Two shells landed in the mud and hissed at the runners instead of exploding. A few more paces and Liebermann fell into a trench. The mud grasped at him and he heard laughing. The beast was dragging him under with comedy, he thought. He opened his eyes to see the hulk of Kluggmann standing over him. He had Lange by the shoulder of his coat and the carrying pole in the other hand.

"I heard that the trench had been blown to hell and I knew

you would get lost. So I came up here and waited. Got everything? What you got for me?" Liebermann pulled out a loaf of army bread. Kluggmann grinned, put Lange down, and picked up the box of grenades. "We need these right away. The rain has taken care of the drinking water problem. You could have left that jug anywhere." He walked off without helping Liebermann to his feet. Lange and Liebermann shouldered the branch with the still suspended water jug. To them the water jug had become a comrade with whom they had undergone a death defying ordeal. They would not let go of it until they had reached their destination. They followed Kluggmann to the dugout. The artillery and mud had missed their prey.

Chapter 6
1500 – 1800

Aflame. A yellow and blue, solitary flame ascended from the wick of a dirty white candle that was stuck into the broken neck of a wine or beer bottle that sat on top of a half meter high grocer's crate upon which one could still read the broad blue label that proclaimed "peaches" to anyone who wondered what had been inside. It was the only light in the earthen underground dugout. The opening, a small cave like entrance, that led to a five step stairwell and the outside could have given the dugout some light but it was covered by heavy brocaded drapes that had once graced a chateau's salon. They had originally kept the cold away from the wealthy and famous. Their new task, in a world of war, was to keep the poisonous gases from seeping into the shelter. The flame, it was almost a bonfire against the darkness, swayed as if it were dancing to some musical phrase which was hidden in each cannon shell's burst that shook the ground above. Its light washed upon near objects to create shadows that also gyrated to the pulses of the detonations. Beyond the shadows only darkness reigned and in it were deadly things.

Half in darkness and half in the shadows Kluggmann, unable to sleep, sat on the dirt floor with his back leaning on the damp earthen wall. He watched the flame. It had become his Lorelei. He could not draw himself away from the rhythmic, swaying movements.

Unknowingly Kluggmann's cannonball shaped head swayed with the flame as if he was her partner. He looked deeply into her shining eyes and down her curving thighs to the small feet that pirouetted on the candle's flat top. He considered where he would put his hands if he had the opportunity to draw her to him. He thought of where he would place the first kiss; it would be a light one. The second, followed by others, would be heavy, passionate, consuming as if he were a drunkard ingesting his first day's drink. His thoughts began to swirl; back to that barmaid in Shanghai, to the black woman in Africa, to the beer maid in Hamburg. Kluggmann wasn't proud. He had paid for his sex in one way or another. Money, gifts, it was all the same but there was etiquette about the transactions. He remembered his manners and wondered how much the house madam would charge him for a night with her. The flame's head dipped as if in submission to his desire. He began forming the idea that he should get up, ask her to dance, and then abandon himself to the swirling music and her arms. But he hesitated. Somehow, in his delusion, he felt that if he got too close to her, she would consume him. Respectfully he kept his distance and admired her shaking and swaying which were made all the more soothing by the three men who accompanied the cannon's beat with a snoring song from a pitch black corner. The men's shapes floated into and out of Kluggmann's peripheral vision as he watched the flame. They were the native band, crammed onto a miniscule stage, which somehow captured the mood with soothing music. They lay close together, closer than lovers sleep on their wedding night for the dugout was not very spacious and extremely cold. There was enough room to stretch out for an average man but the breath was just barely two meters. Neither of the men had a blanket. For warmth they relied on each other's body heat.

A shell exploded above the dugout and dirt fell on the flame ending its life. For a moment, Kluggmann felt remorse that such a beautiful, young woman had had such a short life. He snapped out of his trance and wanted to rush forward to help the lady to her feet so she could continue the dance but he caught himself and instead kicked the boots of the sleepers.

"Time's up. It's time to wake up the rooster." The men did not stir. Kluggmann reached over to the spot on which he had last seen the candle. As he did so he drew out his match carrier. He located the bottle and felt along its neck until he reached the end of the candle. After his vision of the flame as a dancing woman he felt a little immoral as he caressed the wax. He struck a match and in the feeble light he relit the candle. The flame was no longer a dancing woman, it was just a flame. He saw that the men had not stirred so he kicked the soles of their shoes harder. "Alarm!" he shouted and made a commotion about getting to his feet. He threw equipment belts and rattled ammunition boxes. All three men sat up straight and fumbled for their rifles. Lange had already risen to hands and knees. He had become a beastlike animal ready to spring on its prey. The young reach a state of alertness quicker than those just a few years older. Kowalski rubbed his eyes and Liebermann leered daggers at Kluggmann. When the word alarm sunk into Liebermann's cobwebbed laden mind his face changed from a look of vengeance to one of fear. He realized that he was in a dugout, a veritable ready made grave. If a hand grenade was to be thrown in, there would be no escape. He pushed away from both Lange and Kowalski in effort to secure the exit for his own body and disappeared through the heavy drapes. For a brief moment feeble outside light penetrated the darkness and the light of the candle was again extinguished. The darkness added to the panic Kluggmann had caused by his false alarms. Elbows found bodies to poke and booted feet found shins to kick. Everyone, including the perpetrator, was shouting curses. The drapes parted three distinct times as each of the soldiers managed to find them and get them open. Outside, the light of an overcast day greeted them and each breathed a sigh of relief that it had all been a false alarm. Kluggmann, looking like the bratty child who had been caught out, quickly assumed an air of authority to justify his actions.

"You've had your two hours of sleep," he said. "Get up. The artillery is shooting less. Let's go see if we can see any uninvited guests." Liebermann was standing outside the dugout. He was about to lay into Kluggmann about waking him with a false alarm when the sloshing sounds of boots silenced him. Braun had just rounded the traverse on his post inspection to make sure that the watch was being kept by wide awake, alert men. He hesitated about engaging either Liebermann or Kluggmann in conversation but found it difficult to not at least greet them. He felt threatened by the Old Folks just like the others. It was as if the brightness of his personality was somehow dimmed in their presence. There was no reason to ask those two about conditions in front of the position. Their responses were always sarcastic and unnewsworthy. Kluggmann grunted an acknowledgement to Braun's greeting and began to say something but two quick detonations sent all three to the floor of the trench seeking cover from the flying debris. Braun began shrieking and holding his shoulder. Liebermann jumped to his side, pulled Braun's hand away from his shoulder and examined the wound.

"No problem here, Brauney. Something hit you but it didn't break the cloth of your coat. You'll probably have a nasty bruise under there."

Braun refused to get off the trench floor even though the duck-board began to sink from his weight. "I'm hit! You saw it!" He was shrieking like a maddened rabbit just caught in the poacher's snare. His face took on a sullen look as the weight of the supposed wound sunk into his consciousness. His eyes grew to the size of tea cup saucers. He thought out loud. "My god, how will my detachment go on without me?" He quickly dismissed that image and drew out a self serving thought. "I must get to the dressing station before infection sets in. Help me to my feet. Kluggmann, tell Sergeant Brach that he is in command until relieved." He looked down at his feet mentally thanking the stars that both legs were still intact. He regained composure. In a voice that would have been credit to any melodramatic presentation he said, "Tell Brach to report to me at the dressing station for further instructions." Taking on an air of a wounded man who is facing death he continued, "I will join you all again in the rest area if the wound is not too bad. They might order me to the rear. After all senior commanders are well taken care of. " Liebermann looked from Braun to Kluggmann with an astonished expression across his face.

"Look man, there's no blood and no wound. No reason to go back," said Kluggmann as he stepped over to Braun, examined the shoulder which Braun offered up as a puppy might offer his paw when a thorn had lodged there. Kluggmann grabbed Braun by the lapels of his blouse.

"There's nothing wrong with you, hero. Move on to the rest of the posts and put this incident under stories to tell the grandchildren." He shoved Braun against the wall and took up a guard position.

Indignant, Braun responded to the deflating comments, "Are you a doctor, now, Kluggmann?" He stood up straight, in a stance of authority in an effort to intimidate the gefreiter. He winced in theatrically invented pain. The gesture was lost on Kluggmann who was on the verge of laughing when a bullet entered Braun's ear and clanged up against the wall of his helmet on the opposite side of his head. Braun's body slammed against the wall and slid down its semi-liquid side. He sat with legs stretched out the width of the trench, his left arm folded across his lap. One eye had been blown out and lay on his cheek still attached to the tendrils. He gulped at air like a fish out of water and then let out a last exhale. Kluggmann and Liebermann were shocked with the suddenness of the execution but not surprised that it happened. They crouched down to avoid being the next targets but did not remove their eyes from the corpse. Liebermann noted the hole so neatly punched into the steel helmet and reproved himself for thinking that the helmet was any sort of protection. Kluggmann, as always, analyzed the scene before his eyes. He wondered what the gouged out eye saw after it popped out. But the thought was fleeting and was replaced by more practical ideas.

"Go tell Brach he's in charge and ask him when we can go back," Kluggmann told Liebermann. "But before you go, help me push me over the top. Which way is the wind blowing?" They heaved the corpse up on the parados. Two bullets slammed into the corpse at chest level almost immediately. "Damn amateurs out there. Good shots but can't tell a dead one from a live one. Waste of time and ammunition." Liebermann, crouching low, trotted off. Bearing bad news always gave him a thrill especially when it was about someone in authority. Lange came over to see what had happened. Kluggmann signaled him to keep his head down. "Sharpshooter out there has got the door sighted. He has already sent Braun to the hero's rest." Lange displayed no emotion, just nodded and moved off to his appointed place adjusting his equipment straps. He felt for the wind direction and then looked along its path to see Braun's shoulder pointing toward the sky.

"Did you empty his pockets? Get his personal stuff?" Lange asked.

"Didn't think about it. I'll get it later when the night comes. He's already been shot twice after death. There must be a lot of the buggers out there trying to get a medal." Lange shrugged and felt for the packet that contained his last letter. He made a mental note to entrust it with someone soon; but that took courage. Releasing your supposed last letter was the same as putting a pistol in your mouth. Even though these three men were his only true friends, it took humility and pluck to ask someone to take care of what would be his last words. It also took resolve to endure the gentle chiding that would follow such a request. There was always the response: 'you're not getting one of the strange feelings of death are you?' Nevertheless, he didn't want the packet to end up like Braun's personal things; to be gotten later if time permitted and someone remembered. Reassured that the envelope was still in his inside pocket he shivered and took up a position of vigilance on the fire step. The short nap had done him some good but he longed for the warmth that the other two bodies had emanated. It had been so comforting. Kowalski yawned and, and as an exercise at arising, was about to stretch to his full height. Kluggmann pushed him down at the shoulder as a bullet slammed into the trench wall. Had Kowalski risen only a few more centimeters, he too would have had a pierced ear. He gaped at the hole in the wall and wordlessly thanked Kluggmann. He too took up his position at the firing step. "All right. Look alert for the next hour. The fog is setting in. Don't shoot unless you are sure of your target."

Kowalski, a little shaken from the near miss, was not sufficiently frightened to keep from thinking over his position. Silently he mused at how foolish this ritual was of all soldiers being alert one hour before and one hour after twilight. Two hours of all eyes and ears staring and listening for the enemy was ludicrous to a thinking man such as himself. He knew from prisoners that on their side of the line the same ritual was observed at the same time. That meant, to any feeble mind, that an attack would not come at that time because everyone was guarding against it instead of attacking. His lips curled into a smile.

'How ludicrous humans can be,' he thought. Then he thought of all the countless rituals he had read about of which no one knew how they started. 'Maybe a thousand years from now, men will cease working one hour before the sun sets on a particular day and stand looking to the west for two hours and not question why they do it. They will think that their fathers had done it and their grandfathers had done it and countless generations before had done it and not know why.' He almost felt that he could laugh but kept it inside. Involuntarily, one emphatic 'ha' managed to escape his tightly clasped lips. It went unnoticed.

As the sky grayed, flares of many colors arced into the sky all along the line. Some of the brilliant lights hung on parachutes and gently wafted their way to the ground while others ended their existence in their explosions and brilliant flashes of light. As always, the French sent up twice as many flares as the Germans and in such a myriad of colors that many ooed and aahed at the spectacle as if they were watching a fireworks display. In truth, it was the way each side said that they were watching and not to try anything. At this time of day, none of the colors meant anything although in an hour reds, greens, and yellows would be calls for help from the artillery or reinforcements. Many a night, Kluggmann had hoped that someone, just once, would do something when all the men were ready to repel even the strongest of assaults but, as Kowlaski surmised, no one was available for an attack.

Lange opened his rifle's breach and gently chambered a round. For some reason he tried to make as little noise as possible. The call to fix bayonets was relayed along the trench. Metal grated upon metal as the long knives were unsheathed then there was a rhythmic clicking as the bayonet was locked into place on the rifles' barrels. Lange stood leaning against the mud wall of the trench, his rifle across his chest and his trigger figure poised on the trigger guard. Kluggmann peered through a periscope at where the enemy should be. There was no movement. A few shells burst in the reserve areas but otherwise there was an uncanny silence. Everyone, even the sky and earth, were listening. Liebermann, having returned from bearing bad news to the rest of the half company, looked at the parapet where Braun's body was. He could not see the body but imagined the posture it had taken. Braun's muscles had probably contracted and he would appear to be less tall but very flat. Dead men always deflated in the first hours of their new state. It wasn't until much later that they began to bloat although those who had nothing to eat before dying didn't inflate as badly as those who had eaten. He knew that Braun would bloat. He wondered who would have the job of burying him once darkness set in.

The strange silence was broken by a machine gun chattering as another five flares burst high above. Lange noted that the machine gun was a French weapon. To his ear, the French guns were altos while the German ones were baritones. For a few seconds, he marveled at his observation. Congratulating himself for having paid attention to the musical instruction of Professor Higglebaum at the gymnasium. He tried to give a tonal quality to the rifles but was soon shocked to realize that the French machine gun fire had come from a position parallel to his own, where the Bavarians should have been. He became confused as to where the enemy was. Kluggmann had positioned his group to look toward what he thought would be forward but French bullets came from behind and some German shells also exploded behind them. 'Where was the enemy? Were they surrounded?' he questioned himself. A slow panic began to set in but it was quickly allayed when he saw that Kluggmann was calm. The old soldier was setting the pace again. Lange remembered Kluggmann telling them in training that if a soldier gets confused, scared, or questions his existence, then he should look to see what his squad leader or officer is doing. If they are calm, then everything was all right and the soldier should master his emotions and calm himself. On the other hand, Kluggmann had gone on to explain, if the leaders appeared to be scared and confused and showed it, don't follow suit and panic yourself. A soldier should always remain calm. Lange had thought that the advice was too ridiculous. One end of the advice negated the other end; it was a paradox. But, here, among the exploding shells it seemed appropriate. Someone had to be calm. Calmness was the answer to remaining alive and a soldier must find calmness in himself and others.

Brach came around the traverse and went to Kluggmann who intently looked in the periscope. "See anything?" Brach asked. Kluggmann looked at Brach and shook his head. "I wonder if they are even out there," Brach proposed. "Maybe the war is over and those sods have cleared off giving no word to us so that we look the fools still standing here. To them, all this military stuff is a big joke and we're the brunt of the joke." Brach punctuated his observation with a snort that passed as a laugh. Brach was a good egg according to Kluggmann and warranted civil answers and respect. He had been out here since '14 and knew his business.

"A machine gun just shot at us from the flank where the Bavarians are supposed to be," answered Kluggmann. Brach nodded.

"I heard it as I came your way. Better send out a one man patrol to find out if the Bavarians are still there. It's just possible that the French got in the gap between us. If it's just an infiltration the two of us can sweep the area with a crossfire. If the French have pushed out the Bavarians then we're flanked and they'll roll us up as soon as it gets darker. How'd Braun get it?"

"Sharpshooter." Instinctively Brach lowered his frame and darted his eyes from side to side as if his keen eyes would instantly locate a bullet headed his way.

"Where's the body?" Kluggmann pointed. "I'll send someone over to bury him later. I know you and your section are on loan but I really need you to take care of this end of the line. Too many new people to leave it to them. At the first sign of an attack, real or imagined, they'll hoof it. Get some sleep in shifts but stay alert. If they are going to attack again, this is the place." His emotions were beginning to show panic as he thought of more things that could happen. "If they are in that gap and the Bavarians are gone, we're in for it soon." His voice was beginning to take on speed. "We're down to a platoon and a half." He looked about him and saw that Lange was fighting to stay awake. His eyes kept closing and his head more than once dropped to his chest. He wanted to go over and slap Lange but the calmness that lay over Lange's face each time the eyes shut seemed to placate his panic. Lange's features still retained some of the youth that he had seen in his children as he had marched off so many years ago. He continued on with a less stressful voice: "Lucky for us Braun sent for a machine gun section before he came your way. If it gets here in time, I'll send it up to reinforce you. That should give you an edge if they try to rush this end."

Kluggmann nodded to Brach's speech. As each word sank in, he could feel a jolt of adrenalin. A slow state of euphoria was overtaking him. Involuntarily, he began to grin. It was the grin of a wolf. Kluggmann saw that providence had placed him in a dream situation: he saw himself as the single man on the bridge. He was the one warrior who stood between victory and disaster for the rest of the army, the berserker. None would pass him and his men. Brach's final order before he turned and left sunk in over the roar of the adrenaline. "Find out where the Bavarians are."

Kluggmann surmised that he was probably seeing Brach for the last time until they were relieved. Brach was the ranking noncommissioned officer but he had no responsibility to check the posts as Braun had had. The company commander would laud the fact that Brach had taken the initiative to assume command but he would not hold him responsible for the attitude of the soldiers he led. Higher headquarters surmised that without an officer, chaos followed and it was up to each individual of maintain some type of organization as best they could until an officer arrived. Brach would leave the section leaders to do the right thing. When the sergeant's frame disappeared around the traverse, Kluggmann returned to peering through the periscope but not before telling Liebermann to bring the grenade stores out and place them with Lange at the end of the trench.

As the two hours of watchfulness drew to a close, shells of every caliber and description began falling on all areas from the front trenches to the reserve areas. It was a precaution. Command echelons on both sides had told the artillery officers to assume that an attack was under way and that the infantry was too busy to send up signals. They had ordered that each cannon was to begin rapid fire during the last five minutes of the vigil. That last five minute duration was not a period that the infantry man looked forward to. For five minutes exploding shells permeated the air because the shooters, unaware of where the battle line was, simply flooded the area with death. Shells fell long and short. The chance of being killed by one's own artillery increased one hundred fold. All the soldier could do was to push himself up against the trench wall or, if the commander of a particular part of the line was not such a stickler for keeping the men on the fire step until the last minute, seek shelter in the dugouts until the ritual was over and things resumed their normal pace. Kluggmann stayed at his post but sent the other three into the dugout. Lange was grateful since his position had been fortified with boxes of fused grenades. A piece of hot shrapnel amongst the boxes could have spelled his doom.

Darkness was complete when Kluggmann asked Liebermann to fetch the others. Star shells arced in great numbers as each side tried to see into no mans land for sources of noise that were unexplainable. Someone somewhere was always seeing a phantom patrol in the shadows. Even with a star shell hanging in the air and shedding tons of white light over the landscape, a soldier still could misinterpret a barbed wire post for a charging foe.

"I'm going to go on a patrol to find the Bavarians," said Kluggmann to his assembled group. "It seems a French machine gun is either where those lederhosen beer guzzling brains are supposed to be or they're in the gap between us."

"I should go," Lange protested. "I know the way and I made the arrangements." Kluggmann shook his head in disagreement.

"I appreciate the gesture but this patrol needs the hand of an old pro in silent running. Don't blame the Bavarians for the problem. In all this racket and rain, they may have missed the French slipping by. You and Liebermann made a supply run without being seen why shouldn't they be as lucky?" Lange was about to continue his protest when Kluggmann threw a dagger glance at him. Despite their bond of comradeship, Kluggmann was still in charge and to be feared for the authority invested in him by the army and that given to him by his brawn. "Anyway, Kowalski, you poor bugger, is in charge while I'm gone. If I'm not back in say two hours, tell Brach and then get ready for a fight. If they shoot or capture me they'll figure that this is the end of the line and they'll jump at rolling it up." Liebermann looked concerned. He made a mental note that he would stay out there in the trench tonight instead of cozying up in the bunker. Kowalski began to protest about being placed in charge but a sneering glance by Kluggmann shut him up. "Now here's the drill. I'm leaving now. When I find out what I want I'll come back and try to make the end there where Lange should be. My password is whore and the countersign is fifty pfennigs." He paused to remember times gone by. "I always liked a cheap whore."

Chapter 7
1800 - 2100

S odden. The rain continued to fill the air. It was the type a farmer always wished for: thick and steady, without rush, or wind.
Kluggmann slid over the trench rim belly down like a seal slipping
into the sea. The mud washed up over him like a wave coating his
uniform hiding his nationality. Both the French and the Germans
had bombarded that strip of land so much that the soil had turned to
dust. When rain mixed with the dust an oozing, flowing sludge was
formed. Kluggmann let it stream over his hands and face where it
clung to every hair and dived into every crevasse on his pock marked
face. To avoid being silhouetted by the many flares arcing overhead,
he would have to crawl most of the way to where Lange had indicated the Bavarians' positions were located. He wore his overcoat to
give him bulk as well as warmth but he soon regretted his attempt at
self comfort. The rain and mud soaked the coat increasing its weight
and slowing his pace. As a consolation, he congratulated himself on
selecting the lightest weapons to accompany him. A pistol was in his
pocket, his bayonet was in its scabbard on his belt where there were
also six stick grenades tied with heavy twine. He cautioned himself
to deal with anyone he encountered with the bayonet first and then
the pistol. He should only use the grenades as a last resort or when
attacked by two or more. The thought of individual combat was like

reading the menu at a café for him. His mouth watered at the anticipation of adrenalin flowing unchecked through his veins.

The continuous artillery barrage fell on front and reserve positions but none fell in that gap. In his soldier's mind he surmised that the lack of attention to the area indicated that the enemy was there instead of the Bavarians. He turned to look back at the trench to perhaps see one of the Old Folks but the rain, coming from that direction, washed mud from his helmet into his eyes. The momentary loss of vision frightened him. He couldn't use his hands to clear his eyes since they were covered in mud. The result of using them to clear his vision would only have made his vision worse and maybe scratched his eyes. But old soldiers have many tricks. He rolled over onto his back and allowed the rain to wash his face. Sight returned. His heart began to pound quicker in anticipation of an encounter with an enemy.

'Just find the Bavarians. That's the mission,' he ordered himself. 'Killing would have to wait until the trip back.' An inner voice protested and he amended his thoughts. 'But if an enemy should get in my way, you have leave to kill him and then continue the mission.' A piece of barbwire snagged his coat at the elbow. He reached over and unhooked himself and continued to crawl forward. 'Wait,' he thought, 'stick something on that barb to act as a marker.' He reached in his pocket and pulled out the heel of his army loaf that Liebermann had brought from the supply depot. As he attached it to the wire he smiled. 'The bloody thing is not only indigestible, it's indestructible. It will weather better than the pyramids. A thousand years from now one of those museum people will probably dig up that scrap of bread, turned to stone by the ages, and wonder how it got into the battlefield and what its purpose was.' He snorted. The rude noise was a substitute for a laugh.

The dark and the rain obscured his and the enemy's distance vision. The rain also limited the life of the slowly descending flares.

Instead of lasting for long minutes, they went out almost as soon as they exploded to life. The parachutes became saturated and fell on the flare causing it to crash to the ground almost immediately after igniting. If the flares were lucky enough to fall free of the canopy, they burned on the ground lighting up everything at the crawling level. Any rise blocked the ground bound star-like light. Real luck was when the flare landed in a shell hole. Kluggmann crawled on turning his head to the side every so often to allow the rain to wash the spattering mud from his eyes. Lange had told him that the Bavarian placements were less than a thirty meters away on a straight line.

Water began seeping up his trouser legs. The lice, his old friends who infested every part of his uniform, would be frightened for their lives and move further up his body. To entertain himself he wondered if lice were territorial. Would a war break out somewhere near his groin? The upper body lice fighting off the invading lower body lice. Would his balls become a new Morte Homme?

'Crawl on, you fool, he chastised himself. Stay alert and focus on what's around you.' The silt moved about him in ripples. A few more meters and he should be in the Bavarian positions. A new danger arose. How would he convince them to hold their fire? His uniform was indistinguishable from anyone else who was bathed in mud. 'Just scream at them in German', he decided and then he snorted. 'With my Prussian accent they will probably shoot at me anyway.'

Kluggmann sloshed forward avoiding shell holes. The rain puddled in the holes disguised their depth. Often, because of the pulverized soil, a meter deep hole became a bottomless abyss. Those pools, as Liebermann could tell anyone, were mantraps where many soldiers had drowned. Another wire barb tore at his knee. Once again he reached down and unhooked himself. 'Another flag might do well here too,' he thought but he couldn't find anything to hang on the barb. He crawled on giving up the marker idea. The rain had soaked through his overcoat, blouse and vest. It was the closest he had come to an all over body wash in a month. His bored mind resurrected the lice problem. The lice had no where to run to avoid the deluge. Many would drown. He envisioned the tiny newspaper headlines that reported thousands of deaths due to flooding and urged the population to lay twice as many nits to bring on masses that would be needed to reoccupy the body.

At last he saw the first indications of human presence. To his left he could see a wall of sandbags, no more than three bags high and five long. Their skins pierced by bullets and shrapnel bled dirt in small rivulets of sand. Lange had told him that the sandbag wall marked a sap that extended from the main trench. He moved closer to the wall hoping a sentry would not call out an alarm before he was able to get within speaking distance. Then there were voices, at least two voices then a third that grunted rather than spoke. The rain in his ears muffled the sound. The language was indistinguishable. He crawled forward and stretched out against the sandbag wall with his back to the wall. He saw himself as a panther taking advantage of a low rise to conceal himself from the intended prey. But even a panther knew better than to spring before he knew what his victim was doing. He listened. The sounds were still not decipherable. He shook his head to get the water out of ears hoping that the action would make the sounds distinguishable. Then he reprimanded himself. 'Stupid fool,' he thought. 'Don't try to figure out what language it is. Just listen to see if it's German or not.' He took his helmet off. Rain fell on top of his bald head cooling it. He closed his eyes so he could hear well. Finally he surmised that whatever they were speaking was not German even if he compensated for the difference between a Prussian and Bavarian accent. His mission was accomplished. The Bavarians were gone and the French occupied the flank. A deep, throaty inner voice screamed, 'Kill, kill, kill.' He tried to stifle the voice but the beginning of the adrenaline high began to tease. 'Just one or two kills and you can go back. Just one or two kills and you can close your eyes and drift away. Just one or two kills and you can have pleasure.'

Kluggmann quickly and rashly calculated what he could do. Shells were exploding on German and French lines in salvos. The rain was falling. If there were three men in the sap then it had to be deep. Water had probably puddled at the bottom. A hand grenade tossed over the wall would have to detonate immediately otherwise it would roll down the sap's sloping side into the water and explode there not harming anyone. He would have to hold the grenade to the last second before throwing it. The quick explosion would not reach everyone but it would blind anyone too far from the blast and he could take care of them before they recovered their senses. The grenade's detonation had to come at the same time of a shell's explosion to mask it from trench sentries. He agreed with himself that his plan was getting complicated perhaps he could simply crawl away and report what he had learned and prepare his men for the attack that had to come soon. 'Kill, kill, kill.' The need for adrenalin was too demanding. His stomach knotted. His hands shook. The sweat began to form on his brow. He knew from past experience that the pain would get worse and the sweating would become a torrent if he did not act immediately.

Kluggmann untied a grenade from his belt and punctured the tape at the base of the handle. The fuse cord rolled out. For a few moments he looked at the cord. He pulled the cord and the detonator began to snarl. 'Wait. Wait.' A flare arced into the sky lighting up the surroundings. 'Wait.' There was a sharp squeal. A shell exploded. 'Throw.' He reached up and dropped the bomb on the other side of wall. It didn't detonate immediately as he had hoped. There was a shuffle of equipment. 'Not professionals', he thought, 'instead of picking it up and throwing it out of harm's way they're panicking.'

"Mon Dieu!" came from the other side of the wall. The detonation registered as a loud pop like a child's firecracker. Was it loud enough to alarm anyone? There was no time to lose. Kluggmann launched himself over the wall bayonet in one hand and pistol in the other to find only two men. One was dead and the other was stunned and wounded. German grenades were far more effective than French ones. The poilu attempted to raise his rifle but Kluggmann was already on his chest. He slit the wounded man's throat allowing the spurting blood to wash over his hands. The liquid's warmth triggered an adrenalin surge. His heart raced and he heard nothing but its loud thumping. The artillery noise was drowned out. The rain seemed to sizzle on his upturned face. After elongated seconds reality spun itself back into his vision. He crouched expecting an attack from the main line but none came. The artillery explosion had masked the noise of his attack perfectly. Another bit of luck for him was that the sap was not connected to the main defense line. But with good luck comes bad, a shoe taken off and thrown to the floor must be followed by the second shoe. Rifle fire erupted from the German trenches. A sentry had probably seen a shadow move and began firing. The distinctive plop of flare guns gave way to an explosion of colorful lights all along the enemy's trench. Blues, reds, greens and finally a star shell. Their lights didn't last long in the rain but they raised an alarm anyway. There were shouts. Could it be that the grenade's explosion had not been as muffled as he had hoped? The machine gun he had heard from his company's position opened fire accompanied by numerous rifles. Bullets spattered on the sandbag wall inside the sap. Kluggmann flattened himself into the one meter deep depression the former occupants had scraped out. The sap was not built in a shell hole as he had thought. He pulled one of the dead men over him for protection. A thought came to him.

"Arretez! Voulez vous à tuer moi?" Kluggmann shouted. The trick worked. The French stopped firing. Then there were shouts and the noise of clanking equipment coming toward him. He pulled the other dead man to him. Through a gap between the two bodies he pointed his pistol in the direction of the noise. The rain obscured his vision at times. There was nothing that could be done about that. If his trap were to work, he had to remain perfectly still. Soon the top of a helmet appeared. Cautiously, slowly it raised itself above the sap's rim to become a small dome. 'How many were there?' Kluggmann questioned. 'Don't open fire until you know,' he told himself. The helmet became a head followed by shoulders. The rain and darkness were blinding the man. He flicked his head to the side quickly to clear the rain from his vision. The motion made the helmet vulnerable. He was probably wondering what to expect. Did a friend or enemy await him in the hole? Kluggmann had an advantage in that he knew any man who came over the sap's rim was the enemy. The shoulders became a torso.

"Vous etes bien?" the head, shoulders and torso asked. When there was no answer, the mass began crawling into the depression to get a better look. The rain kept Kluggmann from seeing if the poilu was alone. Had only one man come out to see what was going on? Maybe there were two. The other man could be approaching from a different direction. The companion could be behind Kluggmann. Kluggmann's finger tightened on the pistol's trigger before he could stop it and the pistol exploded. The shot caught the man just below the lip of his helmet. His head jerked back with the impact of the bullet. Kluggmann had acted too quickly. Too late the water had cleared from his eyes to show the dome of another helmet on the now dead soldier's left. It disappeared quickly. Kluggmann knew what would come next. A grenade arced into the sap. The two bodies shielded Kluggmann against the inadequate shrapnel. The head reappeared and Kluggmann shot at it. The solid thud noise told him that the bullet had struck its mark. The machine gun and rifles began to fire again. More grenades arced into the sap and once again the bodies protected him. He decided that his best bet of survival would be to act dead. The mud had already made his uniform indistinguishable and the two Frenchmen's blood drenching his coat added to his camouflage. All he had to produce was that vacant stare that dead people did so well.

A man dove into the sap and stuck his bayoneted rifle into one of the dead men. The long bayonet went through the corpse and into Kluggmann's sleeve barely nicking his arm. Kluggmann maintained control and stared forward. The man looked over the corpses and shouted back that everyone was dead. He took the pistol from Kluggmann's hand and admired it. Kluggmann sprang forward like a spider and ran his bayonet into the man's throat and upward into his brain. He looked deeply into the soldier's eyes to see the light go out. He pushed the corpses aside violently, retrieved his pistol and uncapped two grenades which he primed and threw in the direction from which the last Frenchman had come. When they exploded he launched himself over the sandbag wall and laid as close to it as he could. There were a few screams and the machine gun began firing again. The bullets thudded into the sandbag wall on the opposite side. One bullet found a weak spot and forced its way through the bag to clang up against Kluggmann's helmet. It had spent itself getting through the wall and did not pass the metal. The rain and the wall kept him hidden. The machine gun began faltering. Kluggmann reasoned that it would soon stop or give away its position in the darkness. Observers were always looking for machine gun positions. Once they were located, artillery was brought to bear. A few more minutes and he could crawl home. Once away from the sap, he knew that he would be safe. The French wouldn't purse but the star shells would come in their multitudes. They never came into no-man's-land after dark but they were not below firing at shapes in the disputed area. There would be no all fours crawl back. He would have to crawl on his chest back to his own position. Indistinctively, Kluggmann looked at the sky to determine how far away dawn was but the clouds negated any estimates. German shells arced overhead. They sought the machine gun that had so ignorantly given away its location. 'No more delays. You've had your killing. Keep to the path and get back with your information.' How he longed to close his eyes. Not only was he tired but the adrenal had begun racing through his veins. He breathed in pants. His eyes shut and his mind left him for a remembrance of one past deed: when he killed those prisoners in South Africa. He thought about a little nap here against this wall where no one could see him. More shells burst. Had they found their mark? He had to control himself. To stay where he was would be suicide. 'If you want suicide, just stand up. A nap, standing up. It's the same. Stay alert.'

Lange had watched Kluggmann slip into the mud beyond the trench. He wanted to shout out some encouragement but knew that such a thing would be foolish and very dangerous. As he resumed his perch on the fire step, he wondered if that would be the last time he would see Kluggmann's bulky frame. The rain ran in rivers down his back to puddle in his underclothes. Soon they would become sodden also. Involuntarily, Lange shuttered. It was the cold seeping into his very core. Kowalski sat near him smoking his pipe in his one man recess that he had carved into the trench wall. The hole had been spacious for one man to curl up in but the rain was slowly eroding it. The wall in front of Lange was doing the same. The shallow crawl space that they had spent so much time in digging was already flooded and its loose dirt parapet and parados had washed away. They were once again separated from the main trench. If the rain persisted the position's walls would melt away and the threesome would have to find shelter in other less liquidy shell holes. Liebermann had already taken to the parados. It was just as muddy there but he was afraid of the trench floor. The mud wolves resided in the trenches and, he told himself, they had a very good sense of smell. They could trace his presence to any spot and when he was the most comfortable, they would attack by first seizing the soles of his boots and then his pants legs. By being on the parados, they would have to jump to snare him and he would see them coming. He had the advantage. It was true that he was exposing himself to the enemy but the rain and darkness aided him in avoiding detection. To minimize his silhouette on the trench's back wall he had flattened himself so he resembled only a bump on the ground.

Darkness had seeped into every corner of the trench. With the darkness came the cold. May nights still carry the chill of Spring in them. Lange dreaded the cold that would be multiplied by his sodden clothes which already clung to him blotting up any warmth that might come from his own body heat. The only good that was coming out of the rain and the soaking was that the lice were dormant. The persistent itch was gone and his skin was grateful. Kowalski swore.

"Damn rain." He had inverted his pipe bowl in an effort to keep the rain out of it but when he did the tobacco fell out. He had so little tobacco that a sizeable wad could not be built up. He tapped out any remaining sparks and slid the warm pipe into his pants pocket. Aiming at no specific target Kowalski launched into a philosophical diatribe. "The French won't attack in weather like this. Now the British, if they were facing us, would feel right at home in this muck. I've heard tell that England is wrapped in this type of weather most of the year and those Tommies have special eyelids that make it easy for them to see when it rains. Don't believe it myself but some do." He paused to see what effect the statements had. Lange's face was inert. Liebermann's face was turned away so it could not be read. Lange wiped the rain from his eyes and periodically stuck a finger in an ear to clear the moisture. He wondered if his hearing had fully returned. He hummed a few low chords to test his hearing but couldn't distinguish if he heard them mentally or physically.

Kowlaski went on. "The Tommies, I think, are not so different from us. After all, their ancestors and ours are related."

"Yes, professor, I know the histories of England and Germany," Lange said without turning his face toward Kowalski. "But that was over a thousand years ago and since then the Norsemen and the French have mixed with the Saxon blood whereas we have mixed with many other races. The Franks, Huns, Swedes, French even Russians have all had their way with our women over the years. It's a wonder that any one can even say there is a German race. We're more mongrels than the British could ever be."

Not to be outdone by the student, Kowalski found a shred he could expound upon. "Perhaps that is why we are the best at war. Our history is one of struggle. The German people are burned, killed, raped, and starved yet we manage to go on procreating. We have the largest population in Europe."

Lange's voice rose to the challenge. "All mongrels. And please add that we have the most people leaving Germany for other parts of the world where they are not burned, killed, raped, or starved to death. That's how we survive. We transplant ourselves across the world. That's where the purer Germans exist. Those who stay behind hide themselves in forests or collaborate with the occupiers when the forest is stripped of all available food. When the danger passes they come out to profess their nationalism but they don't hesitate to reproduce with anyone near regardless of the nationality. It's as if there is some kind of great haste in replacing those who were lost so they can be prepared for the next invasion or exodus."

"I see what you mean. We fight out here while those at home wait it out safe and sound so they can replace us when we're killed. No shells bursting in Berlin. If we return there will be a different Germany and not the one we are defending out here. A new nation preparing for the next war." Kowalski shook his head from side to side in a gesture of disbelief for what he and Lange had just uncovered. "We're being cheated! We fight on so they can pare down the excess population and get higher wages for less work. They feast on the profits they gain in making weapons that we use for our own destruction and they reproduce so there can be more to slaughter next time. It is a circle of actions which perpetuates itself." He shook his head again and the raindrop that clung to his elongated nose went flying off to rejoin its brothers in the pool that lay at the bottom of the trench. Shells still burst all around as Kowalski sank back against the oozing wall to contemplate his discovery. He had amazed himself. The true nature of the people had trotted itself out of the shrouded stable and neighed in the highest pitch. Kowalski's face showed the amazement. Lange smirked. He had avoided a boring history lesson and given the scholar another mystery to extrapolate over. A German machine gun opened fire in bursts, bursts that sounded familiar. The normal tac-tac-tac had a rhythm to it. Kowalski listened. "Hear that?" Lange thought he meant he had heard someone approaching the trench but Liebermann had heard it to.

"It's Strauss," Liebermann said in a low voice. "Hügel must be at it again. He does that when he is bored. Removes cartridges from the belt to produce a beat. When the war is over he will go far in some band hall as the tuner of machine guns for dancing to." All three laughed, a controlled laugh, but they all thought that at least someone still had a sense of humor in the rain. A French machine gun answered the bursts but not in rhythm. If it were possible, the enemy machine gun seemed to be almost atonal compared to Hügel's gun. "Those Frenchies never appreciate Hügel's attempt at music." The rain had become only a mist.

"My turn at watch," Liebermann said but did not move from his position. "I can see pretty well from up here." Lange slid into a sitting position on what was left of the fire step. The water was already knee deep but, strangely enough, Lange noticed, it was flowing away. The natural contour of the land made a stream. Then he reasoned. True, because the water flowed they would not have to bail it out but on the other hand; the water flowed from the flats all around them into the manmade hole where it channeled itself away. As long as there was water in the fields there would be a stream in the trench. The water would eventually bring down the trench walls and they would be without protection. Liebermann's head came up like a dog that had heard the scratch of a mouse in the basement. He held his breath to hear better then quickly let it out. "Brach's coming over across the top." No one made any effort to look busy or even concerned. The sergeant soon appeared but said nothing. Instead he looked around to see the state of things. He was not one to find fault and let go with curses to the men to fix things. He knew that it was hopeless in their present situation. The only thing he could really do was inspire the men to do the right thing.

"Who's on watch here?" Brach asked. Liebermann grunted.

"Everyone," answered Liebermann and Kowalski supplied the reason.

"It's too damn wet and cold to be sleeping."

"Did you bring us some food?" continued Liebermann whose stomach, as if on cue, let out a very audible gurgle and growl.

"Ration party hasn't come back yet and I wonder if they ever will", Brach spoke directly to Liebermann's stomach instead of his face. "There are so many shells falling that a soldier can't even see a pattern to work around. The lines are so fluid that every time the French stop shelling an area, our guns open on the same hundred meters. I'm quite sure that neither side knows where their men are. They just keep throwing the stuff hoping that not all the shell will go unwasted. Doesn't matter what uniform the victim is wearing. The French must have a rail gun around here too. Big shells go thundering over head toward the back lines every fifteen minutes or so. I'm glad none of them land here." He looked over his shoulder as if he was making sure no one outside the group would hear him. "The big shells land in the back areas where the corps and division staffs have their cozy bunkers and such. I can picture those fat lumps back there scurrying around screaming at how unfair the war is and how they never expected to be under fire. Then they order up some coffee and pastries to calm their nerves." He smiled and giggled like a school girl envisioning what he had just described but quickly straightened himself back into the burly sergeant that he was. "Is Kluggmann back?"

"Not yet," Lange spoke up successfully masking the concern he felt from his reply. "We heard grenade explosions a while back and machine guns chattering but in this rain we couldn't tell if it was near or far. The usual flares went up but just the ones to look around under." Brach glanced in the direction that Kluggmann was supposed to have gone and sighed. He looked around at the trench.

"Looks like you got good drainage here just wish those walls wouldn't melt. I'll have the burial detail bring up some boards to put against the walls," he said in his low authoritative voice. He didn't give a damn that the boards were prohibited. The men needed the protection that the trench gave them.

"Don't bother with the burial detail," said Liebermann. "Braun's body is gone. The mud took it." Brach looked to the parados where he last saw the corpse. The body was gone. "I've been lying up here for quite a while. It must have gone with the flow in that direction." He pointed. Brach looked in the direction Liebermann indicated but the night had blackened that area.

"We'll find him at first light. Even if he was an ass, the man deserves some type of burial. Have Kluggmann find me as soon as he gets back."

Kowlaski asked, "When he gets back, can we leave?" Brach didn't answer and disappeared into the night. Kowalski turned to Lange. "The only way we get relieved is when we are carried back!"

Lange agreed and Liebermann continued his sentry duty without having to agree out loud.

The Germans soon lost interest in trying to find the French machine gun. As if in defiance it loosed a few rounds in an effort to find the cause of worry at the sap. Kluggmann had already crawled a few meters toward home. The rain had subsided. He knew that the lack of rain would bring the French back to reoccupy the sap. He heard the unmistakable clanking of equipment. The poilus muffled their voices but the tones of profanity were obvious. Kluggmann decided to move faster. He shinnied off keeping his face down. He decided again to avoid the shell holes. Even though the rain had stopped, the puddles of water would still be there and just as deadly. He blended in well with the shadows; crawling a few meters, stopping, and lying as still as possible. His overcoat was still sodden as was his uniform. Carrying it was like carrying a full pack but he dared not shed it. The mass provided him with bulk that looked very much like a slight hill when he stopped which was often. Now that the rain had stopped the star shells no longer lost their luster or their momentary height. They seemed to defy gravity swinging back and forth in the slight breeze on their small parachutes scattering their light into every nook and crevasse. The French didn't patrol no man's land at night but they kept it under watch with flares launched almost every five minutes. Complicating the whole picture was that his own army seemed intent on matching the French star shell for star shell.

Exhaustion was closing in on Kluggmann. It was true that he had spent many hours without sleep, food, or water in his career on three continents but that didn't mean he was immune to the weariness that the lack of them brought on. He wondered if he was moving at all. He could still see the sandbag wall. 'I have to set a pace,' he said to himself. Eine, one elbow moved forward. Zwei, the foot on the same side moved forward. Drei, other elbow. Vier, other foot. A cadence developed just like on the parade ground. His body, the main weight, followed the appendages easily enough. He asked himself questions to keep mentally alert. 'How far was it? Could he keep the pace up? Should he rest? Where would he stop?' A flare burst overhead and drifted down on a small parachute. Whoever had fired the round had not pointed the muzzle very high. The flare didn't burn out before it hit the ground. Instead, it landed with a thud and continued to burn lighting up the ground all around. Those types of lights brought machine gun fire because the light projected shadows off all the objects that lay close to it. Barb wire poles became huge and seemed to move in that light. An inexperienced soldier did not see fence pole shadows. Instead he saw an enemy moving toward him and notified the guard who alerted the machine gun crew who fired at the poor defenseless pole. The bullets were deadly not only for the pole but for any soldiers who might be along the trajectory of the bullets. Kluggmann's head, face hidden from the light and eyes closed against the light that would steal away his night vision, felt comfortable with a cheek laid in the mud. He thought of sleep again. It felt so warm, so safe, and so dark just lying there. The light went out and there was no plop to indicate that there was another flare coming.

Kluggmann threw caution to the wind as a short burst of bullets passed him by. He rose to his feet, bent at the waist, and he ran. Where was he going? He remembered a slight dip he had passed on the way over and hoped he was headed in the right direction. The depression would provide cover where he could rest for a few minutes. He wondered how close dawn was. The wind in his face as he ran felt good but, after crawling for nearly an hour, his legs were unsteady and stiff. Muscles cramped sending pains so intense that he thought he was wounded. He listed to one side and then fell over landing with a splash in the mire that was all around. A new string of bullets rent the night but they whizzed far to this right. He reached down to rub the ache away from his lower legs but immediately froze holding his breath. In the light of a new flare he saw the telltale sign of a human: condensed breath rising only a few meters directly in front of him.

There could be no doubt that the person just ahead was the enemy. The Bavarians were not where they were supposed to be and he was the only German outside of this end of the trench. 'It's the sharpshooter!' Kluggmann told himself. The sharpshooter that had dogged his position was in the depression where he had decided to take a rest. 'Probably sizing up his next target. Have to admire the man. Doesn't let darkness stop him from reaping a crop. Shoots by the light of a star shell. But still this one is not too bright. He thinks the darkness totally covers him and because of that he exposes himself. Nothing is totally invisible.' He smiled after the last thought and then curled up into a ball. 'He must have heard me fall. Lay still for a while until he thinks the sound was all in his imagination. Sharpshooters think that common soldiers are too blind to see them. So they lay motionless at any sound assuming the common soldier will pass by none the wiser.' He wondered if his breath was visible and quickly covered his mouth with his hand. The small clouds that the sniper sent out did not diminish. Kluggmann, silently scolded the sharpshooter for his lack of attention to detail. 'Over confident. Foolish. Brash. And a dead man. That's what he is.' Cannon shells were still exploding but the frequency had diminished and their impact was still centered on where the rear areas were supposed to be.

Kluggmann began a debate with himself as his adrenalin level rose slowly. 'Another man to kill. How should I kill the man?' He had no more grenades besides they were too noisy. The deed had to be done silently. That meant the bayonet. Only seconds had gone by since he had fallen but Kluggmann was sure that the sharpshooter's carelessness in concealment was a good indication that the sound had been dismissed as not threatening. The adrenalin began to surge again. It was time to kill the man. Cautiously he crawled toward the breath clouds making his body as flat as possible. 'See what I mean?' he said to himself as if he were looking for approval from an imaginary presence. 'People get foolish in the night. Darkness may be all around but it doesn't matter. That guy thinks he can't be seen.' The wet ground muffled the sliding of cloth across the ground. He froze when he heard the rasp of a rifle bolt as it chambered a cartridge. 'Has he seen me?' He tensed all his muscles and closed his eyes in anticipation of the bullet that would follow but none came. A telltale moment passed. Kluggmann's eyes opened wide when he realized he was not going to be shot. 'He's sighted a target. That's why he chambered a round.' Kluggmann reasoned that the man would be facing toward the company strongpoint and he would have his back to him.

Kluggmann crawled forward ever so slowly. The adrenalin had quickened his heart beat until it was as loud as the artillery. He wanted to enjoy the energy, bathe in it but he knew the real rush would come with the kill. Then he could relax and let the thrill wash over him like a cascade. A star shell exploded and Kluggmann raised his head to chance a look. The light reflected off a rounded helmet covered in dew less than two meters away. The helmet lowered itself. 'He's taking aim.' Kluggmann pulled the bayonet from its scabbard ever so slowly. He did not want metal to rasp against metal. It was insane enough that he would have to move in the light of a star shell. 'I have to move before the shot. He'll move after it. He remembered a stabbing technique he had seen a Chinese boy use against an opponent who had been much bigger than him. He brought his bayonet in his clinched fist up to his chest keeping the blade flat and parallel to it. He saw that little yellow man again, crouching with the knife against his chest and creeping forward. When he had been close enough, he placed the pummel gripped in both hands against his breast bone blade pointed outward as if it had grown from his chest like an appendage. Then he leaped on the back of the victim forcing the knife into the target with the combined weight of his own body and the momentum of the jump. The victim, stabbed through the heart, was neatly impaled and dead instantly. There had been no sound until Kluggmann's shot the man. Kluggmann followed his own description.

The blade, extended like a fang, went into the man's back. Kluggmann's jumping weight drove it directly into the heart area but his weight also collapsed the man's lungs. Evidently he had been holding his breath before shooting. What should have been a muted scream turned into a trumpet of a yell as the victim exhaled. It startled Kluggmann only for a second. He pushed the man's face into the mud to squelch any more cries but it was too late. The alarm had been raised. Another star shell burst and was greeted by a stream of bullets from two machine guns. Both the French and the Germans were firing at the noise. The dead man's body began to convulse. It was as if he were still alive but Kluggmann knew better. His arms flayed about and his legs kicked in all directions but Kluggmann's weight was too much for the dead man to throw off. Kluggmann stayed where he was. The corpse's blood was spurting over his hands. The warmth was indescribable to Kluggmann. He closed his eyes to appreciate the sensation and the sounds of the machine guns. The tacking of the weapons had become the notes of a symphony. He recognized the French gun and there was no mistaking the stop and start bursts of Hügel. He was probably playing another tune. Sometimes the tune was from a stage show that was popular and other times it was some old waltz. Liebermann knew all the tunes that Hügel played on his coffee grinder. When they went to rest billets Liebermann and Hügel would compare play lists. For every rightly guessed tune, Hügel bought Liebermann a beer and vice versa for missed ones. To his credit, Liebermann was rarely wrong and shared the beers with the other Old Folks. Lucky for Hügel the officers never seemed to pay attention.

The sharpshooter's last exhale created bubbles in the slime his face was in and his body deflated. Kluggmann noted that the man was positively boney. He laid as still as the corpse that had become his mattress until the star shells light went out then he pulled his bayonet out of the man's back, rolled off the corpse and lay there to bask in the sensation. The adrenalin pounded in his ears and he felt new energy coursing through his body; however, there was pain. The bayonet's hilt had pushed against his sternum with as much force as the blade had penetrated the man. Kluggmann rubbed the area in an effort to soothe the pain. 'No time for self-pity.' He continued to enjoy the euphoria that spread over his body. The pain in his chest dissipated in the warmth of the flow. 'Got to get back,' he reminded himself. 'Mission accomplished!' He decided to take another chance and hoisted himself to hands and knees. The star shells had all gone out and the machine guns had stopped their exchanges.

Taking into consideration the dip where he had killed the sharpshooter and the sandbag wall, it was probable that he was now hidden from any French eyes. He rose to his feet but kept himself bent in half and began jogging. His right foot stepped on his coat and the rest of his body fell over with a resounding plop. A flare went up. Both sides seemed to be on edge this evening. The flare's light gave him an excuse to pause and allow his muscles to relax. There were no more men to kill. He closed his eyes and drifted back in time. The adrenalin still surged. It was only for a moment. Visions of the past invaded his reality. In his dream he saw himself opening a can of peaches. His mouth watered in anticipation of the sweetness he would find in eating the fruit. The top came away but instead of finding fruit slices he found the face of the grocer from so many years ago. He was startled awake.

Kluggmann's first reaction was to curse the vision but he was shocked to find a piece of army loaf staring into his face. His marker. The relic that would stump the best archeologists in the far distant future. No lights. He rose to his full height and galloped forward.

"Halt, password." It was Liebermann's voice but Kluggmann flopped to the ground. He knew the voice and knew the language but that didn't mean that others around Liebermann were not trigger happy.

"Whore!"

"Fifty pfennigs," came the countersign. "Come on in, you sow." Another star shell burst as Kluggmann raised himself to run for the trench. He had timed the movement incorrectly. The French machine gun chattered; its operator alerted to Kluggmann's running shape. The streaking rounds flew across the ground at lightning speed to strike Kluggmann in both ankles shattering them. He fell head long only centimeters from the safety of the trench with outstretched arms. Kowalski and Lange grabbed each hand and tugged him in as the bullets exploded all along the parapet. Kluggmann thudded onto the fire step chest first, slid over it like a discarded wet towel and landed face down splashing into the water on the trench floor. It was still knee deep. He bobbed to the surface and Kowalski and Lange, laughing, tried to set him on his feet. Kluggmann suppressed a scream and fell back on to the fire step.

"Legs," was all that he could manage to say. Liebermann pulled the legs from the water. He searched Kluggmann's legs from the hip to the ankles where he found the holes in his boots and blood rushing from them. Wounds at the top of the head and ones to the feet always send out more blood than any other part of the body. Liebermann took out his knife and was about to begin cutting the tops of the boots. Kluggmann stopped him. "Idiot! The ankles are already swelling. The boots will stop the bleeding. Just stuff some bandaging in the holes. Help me up." Kowalski pushed his shoulder into Kluggmann's armpit and lifted. Lange tried to steady the standing man but it was to no avail. Kluggmann stood for only a heart beat and fell forward into the water again. All three helped him back to the fire step where he passed out for a moment. Liebermann, stuffed any clothe that came to hand into the bullet holes. The pressure of Liebermann's actions roused Kluggmann and he cursed. He caught his breath. The pain was gone but a stupor began to set in. He was reminded of the first time he had been wounded in Africa. It was a prostitute not a native warrior who had done the deed. He had been seeing her for almost a month and had grown to trust her. He had forgotten that all natives were dangerous. She had stabbed him in the shoulder while he slept. The knife was so sharp that there had been no pain. The wetness of his pooling blood had woken him. Yet he could not get himself up. He watched as the woman stabbed him again almost in the same spot. He wanted so much to grab her hand or deflect the blow but a strange semi-consciousness had come over him just as it was now. He had screamed and frightened the woman who ran away before she could strike a vital organ. He was aware of the same scream and woke from the stupor to clutch at his shoulder. He stared up at the three astonished faces of the only men he had ever called comrades. "The Old Folks have fallen," he sighed and passed out again. Kowalski shook him awake.

"Are the Bavarians there?" he asked. Kluggmann moved his head from side to side. "That tears it. We're flanked."

Brach, after being notified of Kluggmann's information and wounds, sent two stretcher-bearers along to pick up Kluggmann. The stretcher-bearers were dumbfounded when they came to pick up Kluggmann. They displayed a strange demeanor of respect toward Kluggmann gently lifting him on to the stretcher and covering him with a waterproof sheet which they tucked under him as if he were one of their own children being tucked into the mattress for the night. He was no longer the good luck succubus. He was a martyr who deserved an almost religious respect. Before picking him up, one of them warned him to brace himself. Kowalski, Liebermann, and Lange were shocked into wordlessness. Kluggmann did little more than groan and mumble. He roused only long enough to point a finger at Kowalski.

"You. You are in charge," he shouted before lapsing back into the black of his inner self.

Command had fallen to Kowalski who instantly became a fish out of water. He paced about and tried to give instructions but failed. His mouth opened and his lips pursed as if to say something but nothing came out except "me, me, why me?" Liebermann watched him with growing interest. Lange stood back looking in the direction that the stretcher bearers had taken Kluggmann. He wondered what Pfeiffer would say when he found out one of the Old Folks had been wounded. Personally, he felt that with Kluggmann went the four's indestructibility and wondered which one would be next.

Chapter 8
2100 – 2400

Escape. Kowalski felt that he must find a way out. 'Run,' his inner self screamed at him. 'Run before the power of command sucks you into the hell of bourgeois control. No one needs to understand why you're running. Just do it.' His head quickly swiveled to the left, then right and then back to the left. He squeezed one hand with the other in the hopes that he would awake and hear Kluggmann's gruff voice giving direction. He looked over the parapet and imagined that he saw a soldier's back with his hands raised above his shoulders. The gossamer image was walking towards the French lines. A poilu climbed out of the trench as the grey clad figure got close to the wire and he pointed a bayoneted rifle at the soldier. In the last minute before the soldier disappeared into the enemy trench, he turned and looked at Kowalski. The soldier was he. Kowalski nearly screamed and then realized that the vision was a sign of what he should do. All he had to do was get into the darkness and his comrades would lose sight of him. 'At the next near shell explosion,' he told himself, 'in the confusion, I'll slip over the edge and they'll chalk me up as missing.' The only rub to the plan, he reasoned, was that he had to survive no mans' land and a trigger happy enemy that might be anywhere. The classic capture he had envisioned in his waking dream was not the way things happened.

Surrendering prisoners were often shot on sight because of the bother they caused in getting them to the back area. He engaged in such behavior on many occasions. 'No! I can't defect. Too much of a chance of getting killed instead of captured.' His body went limp and his knees buckled causing him to sit on the fire step with an audible plop. 'How dare Kluggmann, in his weakened state, thrust the power to command men upon me. He had no right to do that. He should have told Lange. Although he was young, he is better qualified. Didn't the lieutenant say that Lange was destined for officer training when they returned to the rest areas?' Never in his wildest dreams had Kowalski desired to be in charge of any part of the war. He had been happy to follow, pontificating upon the pros and cons of army leadership. It was so easy to find the flaws and complain about them or wax over the good when things went right and he was well fed. In either case, he took no personal instruction from the faults or goods. Like so many of his philosophical colleagues he had no solutions to the flawed system or a way to keep the better methods from deterioration.

'Where did I go so wrong?' Kowalski asked himself. 'Could Kluggmann have believed all that petty reasoning? Did he believe all those stories about my participation in the unions? As a former mine worker he reveled in those tales of standing up to the bosses.' Yes, it was true that as an active socialist, he had participated in strikes and protest marches but he had always felt content to follow, mouthing the words of contempt that the mob chanted. The only leadership he had shown in the labor movement was through his booming voice. Its tones had helped in motivating those who faltered. But it was his way to be a follower and not a leader. Brach added more pressure to his burden by sending over three no-name soldiers to reinforce the position. Horror upon horror. Five people looked to him for instructions and guidance in staying alive for the next moment; two of them were his very good comrades whom he would not be able to give orders to. They would laugh at him and the no-name soldiers would have no confidence in his leadership.

'Run', his inner self shouted again louder than before. He looked at Lange to see if he might have heard his throughts. They seemed to be so loud. He shook his head, 'can't run. Have to stay. Have to become a leader.' Then the answer to his dilemma came to him. His superior, intellectual, inner voice interrupted his fight or flight reaction. That was the voice that motivated him. It had never been wrong. 'The experience will make you more valuable to the party when the war is over.' He smiled. There had always been a reason for crises in his life. He had only to reason them out to find why they were happening to him. He congratulated the voice within on having such keen insight.

The wounding of Kluggmann had removed the stigma and fear of the Old Folks. The new no-name soldiers were proud to be with the Old Folks. They pranced about like puppies who try to please the leader of the pack. They were grinning and emanating sounds that sounded like laughing yelps. Each, it was evident, wanted to be Kluggmann's replacement. Kowalski removed his helmet to smooth his hair in a comforting way and became acutely aware that his hair, although only two centimeters long, was falling out. He wanted to pluck out a few strands to see if they had already turned white from the worry that seemed to consume him as never before. Indecision. Indecision. Just a few hours ago he was digging a trench and cursing. What would Kluggmann have done if he, Kowalski, had been taken out? He suffocated a laugh although a smile did cross his lips. The answer was, do nothing. Kluggmann would have shrugged his shoulders which may have meant that he didn't care who got hurt or that he saw wounds as inevitable. Either which way the first words out of his mouth would have been:

"All right! Take up your positions!" Kowalski said in a low, commanding voice to the five men who lay about. Had he been on the receiving end to the order he would have heard a tone that very near-ly asked rather then demanded. Perhaps later as things developed he would have the time to listen to himself and modulate where needed. How well he knew that tone was everything in speech mak-ing and handling men. Consciously he stifled any hand movements. He was now a figure of interest to any sharpshooters in the area. Directional hand movements are a dead, no pun intended, give away as to who is in charge. He glanced around thinking that he would see a rifle muzzle pointing at him. He saw no one but his five charges who were looking at him rather than watching for the enemy. "Eyes front. Watch for the enemy. I haven't any in my pockets!" Sarcasm! How very appropriate. He congratulated himself. The five heads snapped to look in other directions. Neither of them knew where the enemy was so any direction was as good as the other. Looking at the backs of their heads his more timid, primitive inner self tried to take control. 'Run!' Loud again. 'They won't even know you're gone for the few minutes that it will take you to reach the darkness.' It was not the voice that directed him with reason. These tones came from his primeval self. It was because of that voice that he was only a fu-silier. It had kept him from achieving more. He forced the voice into a deep recess and took control. "Liebermann, we need some fresh water up here. Rain water won't do. Go see if any can be spared."

"But I'm on sentry for another thirty minutes," Liebermann whispered back hoping that others would not notice Kowalski's mis-take of assigning duties to a sentry. To Kowalski there seemed to be a mocking in its tone. In his very short tenure as leader he had be-come aware of the resistance followers showed to even the slightest direction to control them. Kowalski needed to show that he would not back down from a decision.

"One of the new people will cover for you. Go do as I ask." Kowalski pointed to one of the no-name soldiers who sighed and made a comment under his breath at which his comrade laughed.

"What's that? I didn't hear you," asked Kowalski menacingly. Everyone was against him now. He mentally padded himself on the back and thought: 'It's lonely at the top.' The soldier grunted and turned to put a foot on the fire step but the saturated dirt gave way under his weight and he fell face head first into the parapet. Kowalski's inner self roared with laughter as his outer self showed a grimace of disdain. The soldier picked himself up spitting mud and assumed the stance of vigilance. Liebermann went off to find some water.

Lange went down to the end of the trench and sat on the fire step with his back to the trench wall. The grenade boxes they had stacked at that trench end had gone undamaged by the artillery barrage. He used one of them as a foot stool. The other two soldiers began excavating one man fox holes in the side of the trench. They gave up after a few strokes because the wall did not hold. The soil was still saturated from the day's rain and loose. They sat on the fire step which had become rounded through erosion and no longer than a foot in length. A waterproof sheet on their bottoms kept the moisture away from their uniforms. One of them began asking questions about Kluggmann. How long had he been a soldier? Where was he from? Was it true that he had been a trained killer in Africa or was he a demented former insane asylum resident who had become patriotic? Lange, at first, answered a couple of questions but as the idiocy grew he became irritated with those no-name soldiers. Shells were still exploding all around them. Lange hid his growing anger by signing to the no-names that the noise didn't allow him to hear them any more. The feinted excuse soon became reality. Three shells crashed to earth not far from the trench. Lange cursed as the torrent of mud displaced by the explosions splashed over him.

Wiping the mud from his face, one of the no name soldiers shouted, "Hey, those are from our cannons!" Lange shook his head. He knew that the quantity of explosions around them made

distinguishing whether it was German or French shells that exploded on either side of their position was impossible. The gunners were
as confused as the infantry man was as to the location of the front
lines. But he was above explaining that to the no names. They would
have to learn by themselves how much of an insignificant thing they
were to the wielders of the manmade lightning bolts.

"There's someone coming," whispered the sentry.

"Where?" asked Kowalski.

"Along the trench. Halt. Who's there?" Lange and the others
chambered rounds and prepared to fire into what might be a French
raiding party.

"It's your saviors," said a lilting, Rheinish accented voice.
"Machine gun detachment ordered to bolster your defense."

"Come on." A gefreiter came out of the gloom followed by four
men carrying the weapon and the equipment needed to operate the
gun. Kowalski looked relieved. The sight of the man's rank meant
that he could relinquish his leadership role. A huge weight came off
Kowalski's shoulders. He felt that he could defy gravity. Involuntarily
he smiled and put his hand out to shake the gefreiter's hand. But before contact could be made, his euphoric cloud disappeared.

"We'll set up over there," the gefreiter told Kowalski and indicated the area where Liebermann had lain on the parados. "That
position will give us a good cone of fire if an attack develops. Your
position will give us rifle support covering our flank. You watch over
your men and I'll take care of mine." Kowalski tried to object but the
five men crawled up on the parados and disappeared into the inky
dark. In a moment, Kowalski could hear shoveling. The crew was
digging in. Kowalski was still in charge of the riflemen. The weight
of responsibility, doubled since he had let it go, came crashing back
on his shoulders.

The magic of the Old Folks was gone. Lange felt a new sensation
flood over him. It was not apathy or even depression. It was one of

retribution from the fates. He questioned himself about a possibility of atonement for the many times he had laughed at others' bad luck and reveled in his own good luck. He reasoned that if the fates had taken one of the Old Folks would they take more? Unconsciously he felt his breast pocket to make sure the letter he had written to his mother was still there. He had wrapped it in a bit of waterproof sheet to keep it safe from rain or his own blood. With the letter were things he felt as being personal: a cigarette lighter that he never used, money that he had saved for his next furlough, and a crushed flower that reminded him of youthful, carefree days. Elsa had given him that flower when they were children, aged not more than nine or ten. He had kept it safe all these years wrapped in tissue paper in his wallet. True he had forgotten of its existence as he had grown older but, miraculously he had found it the day before reporting to the regimental depot for training. He had selected Homer's Iliad to take along with him to the barracks and the flower had fallen from the pages as he took the book from the shelf. His heroic youth's mind had thought the shade of Achilles must have pushed it from the pages. A moment of melancholy stole through Lange's thoughts as he considered the contents of the small bit of waterproof sheet. That miniscule packet was all of his personal life. He wondered if other people his age had so simple of a life that they could wrap it all in a piece of material that wasn't more than a few centimeters square?

Lange wondered who he would entrust the package to now that Kluggmann was gone. He thought he heard an inner voice say that he should give the parcel to someone immediately. He rose to his feet but the distinctive plop sound of a trench mortar being fired stopped him. He looked up to see the huge round object lit up by an exploding flare arcing, its path given away by a tail of sparks, toward him. The sparking shell reminded him of a shooting star. Involuntarily, he made a wish on its tail and then snapped back to being the soldier.

"Take cover!" Lange screamed but continued to watch the shell reach its peak where it was lost to sight as the flare died. He was transfixed to the spot. Death was in that shell, his own death. A star shell burst distracting him from the mortar round. It lit up the objects around him. The no-name soldiers were rolled up into little balls clutching their rifles while Kowalski stood looking at him with an expression that could be described as dumbfounded, clueless as to what should be done. Lange, seeing visions of his dismemberment took the opportunity of command as offered. "Stay calm," he said to Kowalski in a tone that reminded him of Kluggmann. "In the last light I saw where it was going. It's headed away from us." The sound of an earth shaking explosion came just moments after Lange's reassuring words. Kowlaski's expression turned to one of relief but the one of fear soon returned as five more distinctive mortar plops were heard. The trench guard's alert added to the atmosphere.

"There's movement coming our way!" the guard shouted. Kowalski jumped to the guard's side. Kluggmann's training was working. He reasoned that the short barrage was a clarion to a trench raid. He must post the men to receive the attack. The incoming mortar rounds were forgotten. There was nothing he could do to stop them but he could try to stop the attackers.

"Where?" Kowalski shouted. The guard pointed to the gap Kluggmann had just recently crossed. Kowalski estimated that there was a half a company on the move in their direction as the light from the star shell finally faded out. In the direction of the machine gun detachment, Kowalski shouted, "To the right at twenty meters. A platoon." Inwardly he chastised himself. In what direction was right for the machine gun crew. He heaved a sigh of relief when he heard the gun's tac-tac and bullets whizzed over his head in the right direction. "Lange, throw some of those bombs at them. The rest of you open fire to the right."

The mortar bombs began exploding. A strong wind followed

each detonation which nearly toppled Kowalski. They had missed his position. Mortar rounds were not like artillery rounds. Cannon shells, whether high explosive or shrapnel, seemed almost surgical to mortar rounds which weighed as much as ninety kilos. Their operators did not aim their shots. They simply pointed the barrels in the direction of the enemy and hoped for a good outcome. The shells' explosions were deafening and the shock was devastating. Kowalski had seen men disappear in their blasts or, if the detonation was close, strip a man of his clothes and toss him meters away, his insides turned to pulp. However, their deadliness was outweighed by the fact that a soldier could see them coming and get out of the way if possible. A traverse was the best protection. Bunkers were death traps because of the mortar's violent explosion. Roofs would cave in under them burying those inside.

Two trench mortar rounds exploded along the left. Kowalski watched as men and equipment flew into the air and flopped down with a sickening crunch. He wondered why the machine gun crew was no longer firing.

"You!" he shouted at one of the no-name soldiers, "Go tell that machine gun crew to continue firing into the gap. They're going to get in there and attack us from behind." The soldier raised his head and momentarily looked around at the exploding shells. He shook his head and rolled up in a ball in the two inches of water at the bottom of the trench. Kowalski grabbed his arm but was unable to pull him out of the position. For a second he considered what he should do if men refused his orders but he quickly ruled that out. Killing a man without the provocation of it's him or me was impossible for him. Before he could turn to another man, Liebermann appeared with a machine gun across his shoulder and one water bottle.

"They're dead," Liebermann said without ceremony or expression of remorse. It was the Kluggmann shrug. "Mortar blast. It got the gun crew but the weapon still works. You," he pointed to one of the no-name soldiers, "get the stand and ammunition. It's down the trench about two meters. Lucky for us the whole thing was blown into the trench instead of out of it." The soldier came back grunting with the equipment. Another soldier took the water canister from him. Lange set up the gun and loaded its first belt. There was no time to camouflage the gun. The white flash of the first rounds would give their position away immediately. Lange cautioned himself that he should fire in short bursts to limit the flash then he thought about to where he should move the gun after a few belts. Their space was very limited. Kowalski sent up a flare not only to see if the enemy was still advancing but also to cover the light that would come from the discharge of the machine gun. In the dim light he saw the movement.

"There. Twenty meters." The machine gun rattled. Liebermann had gotten hand grenades. He fused them and threw. One of the no-name soldiers assisted him, fusing the grenades and handing them up to him to throw. Six of the enemy had fallen in the first machine gun burst but it was impossible to tell it they were dead, wounded, or just seeking cover. Darkness covered the bodies when the flare's light faded out. Kowalski kicked the no-name soldier who was still curled into a ball on the floor. The other no-name just fired aimlessly in the direction of the gap. Kowalski shouted at him. "Pick a target, you fool. You're wasting ammunition." He ignored him and loaded another clip into his magazine before blazing away at the stars again. Lange slapped the machine gun's receiver with his left hand and the gun barrel moved a few inches over to spew bullets in a new cone of death. He let off another twenty shots. A few more of the enemy may have fallen. The distinctive dull thud of a bullet hitting a body was a sound Lange knew quite well but he was hard pressed to say if he had hit more than one person. He slapped the receiver again. Another twenty shots and a slap to the right. He knew he was forming a pattern that might be perceived but it was the only way to cover the whole area and not give away his location.

Some of the assault party had taken refuge in a shell crater and were firing toward the machine gun's flare. Liebermann tried to arc his grenades into the shell crater but he wasn't succeeding. Kowalski stopped Liebermann. Throwing grenades with the hope of landing them on target was a waste. They both knew that the enemy was out there. Rifle bullets were whizzing over their heads but they were too far away to be reached. One of the no-name soldiers screamed and rolled to the trench bottom. The soldier who had been nearest to him jumped to his aid but Kowalski stopped him.

"We're under attack. Leave him. Keep firing," he admonished the man. The no-name wanted to protest but Kowalski pointed his rifle at him. This time he would shoot if the order wasn't obeyed. The body hit the lump still curled in a fetal positon on the floor. A hand reached out and touched the wounded no-name. It groped for a few seconds. Then the body uncurled. The no-name chambered a round and jumped to the fire step beside the still firing comrade. In ten seconds, his ammunition was spent and he reached in his pouch for another clip he looked in the direction that his friend had rolled. He could distinguish a body but there was no sound. Was he dead or unconscious? A deep sigh and then he put the strip in the open chamber, pushed down, loaded a round and continued firing. Kowalski had watched the scene open mouthed. The fear of mutilation by shells could freeze one's marrow but an exchange of bullets could bring fanatical courage. Kowalski joined the two adding the fire of his rifle.

Lange knew that he would have to move the weapon after the next burst or the trench mortar would get him. Someone, some-where, was doing the mapping based on the flashes. Another slap to the receiver and a short burst. He didn't want to burn up the barrel or exhaust the water since he had neither to replace the loss. Lange turned to the others who were blindly shooting into the gap.

"Let's move it!" Lange picked up the gun and water case while the others got the rest. Liebermann was already stuffing grenades in his pockets. The no-name soldiers looked to Kowalski who nodded. They ran down the trench to Brach's bunker as mortar bombs arced overhead. A traverse protected them from the explosions. Lange pointed to where the stand should go and reset the gun. He fired into the position they had just left and elevated the barrel to shoot beyond. Kowalski and Liebermann fired in the same direction. The no-name soldiers were also firing but their support was faltering then they stopped.

"What about Miller?" one asked. "We left him there."

For a moment, Kowalski allowed his mind to ask who Miller was then he remembered the man who had been hit. A sarcastic answer came to Kowalski's mind but he suppressed it. "Too late," was all he said. "Keep firing!" The men chambered rounds and fired. An artillery round burst at the same time they fired startling everyone. German shells began falling in front of their positions. They took cover in Brach's dugout rather than continue fire. Lange, gave the machine gun to Liebermann. He shouted into Kowalski's ear and disappeared down the trench. In a second he returned.

"We're the only ones left up here," Lange shouted. "Brach and the others are gone. They probably hightailed it to the reserve position when the mortar bombs began to fall. We have to get out of here!" They began running down the trench toward the communicator. Liebermann led the machine gun on his shoulder. The no-names wanted to abandon the machine gun's equipment and ammunition but Lange forced them to pick it up with a few wallops to their ears. Kowalski became rear guard. The mortars had blown in most of the trench in front of them. The only route they could take was across the open ground. The noise of bursting shells and the hot acidic wind that followed was unnerving. Lange and the others were lifted off their feet by the winds many times but they scrambled to regain their feet motivated by the fact that they were not protected by thick earthen walls. At times it seemed the entire world was exploding and they were the only living things to stand on firm ground. They rushed aimlessly into the darkness guided by a desire to stay alive. Then Liebermann stopped and stood looking around him.

"I'm lost!" he screamed trying to make his voice heard above the din of exploding shells. Lange tripped on a piece of barbed wire that was still fastened to its buried post and fell. A shrapnel shell burst overhead. There was a scream and Liebermann fell across Lange. The weight of the machine gun added to Liebermann's weight almost broke Lange's back. Relief came when the machine gun rolled off Liebermann but he was still pinned to the ground. Lange swore and tried to get out from under Liebermann but only managed to raise his head as another shrapnel round burst. He could hear the bullets slamming into Liebermann's covering body and into one of the no-names that lie beside him. The no-name's body was pushed into the ground by the explosion and shrapnel so violently that the mud splashed to a meter's height around him. Lange, under Liebermann, began shouting for Liebermann to get off him but Liebermann did not move. Lange heaved his shoulder upward moving Liebermann slightly. Kowalski tugged at Lange freeing him from beneath Liebermann with the help of the fluidity of the mud.

"Are you hit?" Kowalski asked.

Lange shook his head then turned his head to Liebermann. "Are you wounded?" he asked Liebermann. But Liebermann's voice did not answer. Instead, he gurgled. Kowalski rolled Liebermann over. The rim of the helmet hid his face. Kowalski threw the helmet to the side to see that most of Liebermann's face was gone. Shrapnel balls had somehow avoided his helmet but destroyed his face. He had probably never felt the second round that had torn into his back. For a moment Lange and Kowalski sat staring at Liebermann. They were oblivious to the continued shell explosions around them. A star shell's light burst over the landscape and Lange and Kowalski had one last clear look. In that last look they took leave of Liebermann without saying a word. He was dead. No tears. Just a look. Liebermann had escaped whatever the world would go through after that moment. He had the luck whereas everyone else had come in second. As the light faded Lange saw to the no-name soldier who had fallen with Liebermann. He was dead also.

"If we leave them here, the mortars will keep tearing at them!" Lange shouted at Kowalski who nodded. To simply leave Liebermann and the no-name to such a fate seemed sacrilegious. The two of them grabbed Liebermann's harness and dragged him along to the nearest shell crater. It was half filled with water and they could see that the puddle had no depth. They stuck a rifle at the rim and let the body slid down the crater's side into the puddle at the bottom. Curiously the body did not disappear at once. The muddy water seemed to open like a mouth that pulled the body into its depths as if there were unseen teeth that inched along the length of the corpse. It was if something below had swallowed him in bites. Then a large bubble broke the surface and sounded like a burp. The no-name's body received the same burial. Lange retrieved the machine gun. Kowalski and the last no-name soldier hefted the equipment. They ran into the darkness.

The darkness was all consuming. There was neither north or south or any other direction but straight ahead. Kowlaski was leading with the no-name soldier bringing up the rear. The mortar bombs had stopped falling and the cannon rounds were tapering off. Fire often dropped off around midnight and remained relatively silent for a few hours. There were always machine guns chattering and a few big caliber artillery rounds screamed over head going towards the back areas. It gave a front line soldier a sense of satisfaction that the common folk who loaded and shot the big cannons were making fat colonels and generals dodge rounds in the back areas where they thought they should be safe. Yet it was a shame that those backline people would count the one round that got close to them as a barrage and put themselves in for bravery under fire medals.

Lange lifted his head to see if he could get a bearing. Star shells burst here and there. They threw themselves down and hoped they were not seen. Destroyed trenches had forced them to go along open ground for the last fifteen minutes. The going was easier but very risky. They stumbled along sometimes at a run and other times at a crawl. Lange's head swam with a fog that muted all desires and intentions. Somehow he managed to get one foot in front of the other. Only once had he fallen into a shell crater. Lying on his face had been so blissful that he had snarled at the two men who tried to help him out of the hole. He had recognized Kowalski and allowed him to help him up but he would not let the stranger touch him. Finally he had got to his feet but the first step had been so painful. Every toe seemed to shriek as he tried to run. The weight of the machine gun on his shoulder was almost too much to bear. Why didn't he throw it away he asked himself. But, he reasoned, how would you protect yourself? He had lost his rifle. The thirty kilo gun was the only thing he had to say he was still a soldier. His uniform, so caked with mud, had lost all semblance of being an identification of sorts.

The machine gun seemed to be cutting through Lange's coat and into his shoulder. Kowalski saw the pain, stopped and exchanged loads with him. Lange took the gun carriage in exchange for the gun, not much of a difference. He lifted his head as if he were looking to the heavens for help or relief. When no help came he steeled his gaze on what he thought was the horizon. In the distance he was sure he saw a muted glow. 'Is that the angel of death nearing?' he asked himself. His body seemed to become lighter almost at once. 'Am I about to be freed of this accursed body?' He squinted to clear his eye sight. The glow became brighter as he approached it. He tried to pierce the glow. Would he see an angel's or a devil's face?

Another squint and the glow showed itself to be a tangle of vines. It was the tree's roots that he and Liebermann had passed earlier that day. Beside the roots he could see the ruins of the communications trenches. "This way," he motioned and led the way mimicking the pace he had learned from Liebermann. In a few paces, the muddy, filled in trench gave way to a deeper cut lined with boards. They let themselves into the two meter deep trench with relief actually splashing in the knee deep water as children might in a mud puddle. All three wanted to relax for a while, catch their breath but Lange led on. It was as if Liebermann was leading him. They came out of the trench and saw the destroyed wood ahead where the rest of the company lay hidden. There was a pause to catch their breath and congratulate each other on making it. The no-name took on a name. It was Schneider. Kowalski stepped off and he was greeted by three rifle rounds that whined over his head. He fell flat, the machine gun almost crushing his back.

"Who's there?" came a familiar voice. It was Brach.

"It's father Christmas and his two helpers. We've got some coal for your black heart. Quit shooting at us!" Kowalski answered.

"Come ahead!" The three of them sprinted to the fallen trees and into the shelter of a covered trench. Lieutenant Pfeiffer greeted them.

"Where have you been? We gave you up for dead a long time ago. Lange, you brought a machine gun out! You men will get a medal for this. Our machine guns were destroyed." He was slapping Kowalski, Lange, and Schneider on the back and almost dancing a jig. Everyone stared at him wondering if he had snapped. Quickly the lieutenant regained his soldierly face and had the other company men take the gun and set it up. Kowalski collapsed to the ground but Pfeiffer helped him up. "Kowalski, you deserve promotion. You are a gefreiter from this moment on. Take a rest and then take over the second platoon, first section." Kowalski grimaced. "Are the French behind you?" Kowalski reported on all that had happened since Kluggmann was wounded. Pfeiffer kept his face down taking in the information. When the report was over he shouted orders to prepare for an attack. Then he turned. "Lange, go lay down in my dugout."

Lange stumbled along the trench counting the number of openings. Finally he reached the company headquarters. He pushed aside the heavy drape that covered the dugout entrance and stepped into a darkness that grabbed hold of his very essence. His eyes rolled to the top of their sockets and the lids slammed shut. There was coolness about the darkness. He didn't want to open his eyes to try and see where he could lay. He fell forward as a limp sack of flour. There was a human shuffling in front of him but his closed eyes could not see. There was a grunt and a few curse words but Lange ignored the harshness. He was asleep.

Chapter 9
2400 – 0300

Darkness. Kowalski found himself swimming in a black sea over which hung an equally black sky. There was neither a moon nor stars. Without any light, the water, its presence betrayed by occasional foam capped waves, and heavens merged into a dimensionless darkness on the horizon. The cool water that lapped about him felt refreshing but in its depths there was no comfort. His arms moved mechanically, one over the other. His hands scooped the water away from in front of him effortlessly but yet it was a tedious endeavor to keep going. He wanted to stop and float to rest just for a few moments but something drove him on. He became annoyed as each stroke forced the water over his ears deafening him and into his eyes blinding him. Yet he could not stop. It was if his arms were part of a perpetual motion machine. He barely caught his breath before he reached out into another stroke and the water lapped up over his head again. 'Where am I going?' he asked himself. Questioning himself broke the machine's action. His arms went limp and he bobbed in the water like a fisherman's line cork. The water's waves buffeted him from side to side. An occasional wave managed to lap over his head as if it were attempting to keep him blind and deaf. He fought the waves off and wiped his eyes. His vision cleared. Ahead of him he could see where waves crashed on sharp, sheer rocks. He marveled at the height that the sea foam rose as each wave, dying in a thunderous roar, dashed itself against the granite like surfaces. For a moment he felt relief that there was land within sight but then he realized how dangerous his position was. He reasoned that if he got nearer to the shore the waves would pick him up and hurl him toward those rocks. He would be powerless to stop himself from being crushed as the waves threw him again and again against the rocks. Already the undertow was tugging at his feet. He began back paddling with the intention of swimming along the coast until he found a better place to get ashore. 'Will I have the strength to make it?' he questioned himself. In response he heard his inner guardian voice whose advice he found so reasonable. 'Better to drown than be crushed.' Mockingly it continued by asking, 'Just how many times would the waves force you against the rocks until death came? Surely the first collision would not kill. You would have to endure the pain many times before death came. Yes, better to drown than die a slow agonizingly violent death. Just open your mouth and gulp the water as if it were air.' It was then that Kowalski heard other voices. They were faint but their volume rose until it drowned out the waves beating against the rocks.

"Kowalski, what do we do now?" they shouted at him. He looked to the right and then to the left. There among the swelling waves were ten helmeted men holding rifles above their heads. They bobbed on the water as he did, fisherman's line corks. "Kowalski, what do we do now?" they repeated in a tone that seemed to echo off the nearby cliffs. The booming surf grew louder as if competing with the voices around him. Kowalski looked from the heads to the shore. He was nearing it. The current was getting the better of him. He was being pushed toward the rocks at an alarming speed. Eddies were forming and he feared being sucked into one. He looked to the men and warned them of the danger of following him but they would not break away. He looked to the rocks again to determine if there was a niche in them into which he could safely lead the men. The sea foam towered above him and the noise finally drowned out the men's pleas.

"You're in over your head," said a voice from above. Kowalski wiped his eyes again and looked in the direction of the voice. For a moment he wondered about the existence of a supreme god then he saw a wooden boat riding the waves just centimeters away. In it was Kluggmann. "I repeat, you're in over your head," he said glaring at Kowalski with those pale blue eyes as he had done many times in training when he found that Kowalski would not obey the instructions. There was coldness in them. They stared at him as if he were prey. Kowalski grabbed at the side of the boat but Kluggmann rapped his knuckles with an absurdly small oar. It was not more than a half meter long. "No room here!" Kluggmann shouted. "You'll have to make do by yourself. I can't keep giving you a bail out every time you get in trouble. Ha! Good joke! Get it? Bail out!" With that said, Kluggmann, with the two small oars began rowing away. Neither blade actually touched the water yet the speed they generated was extremely rapid.

"Wait!" Kowalski yelled but Kluggmann pulled away and into the surges that sent the water crashing on the rocks. Kowalski watched helplessly as the waves seized the boat churning it as if it were a leaf going into a sewer grid and then rammed it into the rocks. Kluggmann and the boat debris shot upward into the foam. Kluggmann's faced almost appeared to be smiling as his body disappeared in the greenish whiteness of the surf. Kowalski wanted to shout but the water washed into his mouth.

'Let the water take me then,' he whispered to himself. The undertow was tugging at him furiously. The men had reappeared and were calling to him for instructions. The surf's thunder grew louder. He felt the waves take control of his body and begin forcing it from side to side. The water pushed him down and tossed him head over heels. He couldn't catch his breath. He tensed his muscles in anticipation of the rocks' surfaces.

"I've found Kowalski!" a familiar voice broke through the meters of water that Kowalski had sunk under. Kowalski opened his eyes as a man cleared away the water that had strangely turned to dirt and wood debris.

"Alive or dead?" another voice asked.

"I'm alive!" Kowalski answered in rasping tones. Someone cheered. It was Brach. Lange pulled at Kowalski's arms as Kowalski kicked furiously to free his legs. One foot came loose but the other seemed to be tied down or held. He looked down to see what held him so fast. It was a bloody corpse. For a moment Kowalski shuddered. Was it the devil grasping at him or just a dead soldier whose arms somehow had got entwined with his legs? He kicked at the mangled mess with a freed left leg. Neither the devil nor a dead man deserved niceties. The mass gurgled and seemed to grasp him even tighter. He kicked again and the corpse gave way.

"Looks like you're the only survivor, man," said Lange as they stood side by side surveying what had once been a dugout. "The shell exploded directly above your bunker and collapsed the roof. If it had penetrated before it exploded we would have filled in the hole and marked your grave." Kowalski still oblivious to the world around him automatically picked a rifle out of the debris and examined it to make sure it was still workable. He marveled at how the weapon had survived and the humans had not. Lange shook Kowalski's shoulder in an effort to get his attention. "Any idea how many were in there with you?" Kowalski looked at Lange. The question sunk into his consciousness. He moved his head from side to side and regretted the movement. It felt as if his brain moved from side to side independent of its casing crashing into the skull at tremendous speed. The pain that the collisions caused a pain that sent tremors through his body and attempted to buckle his knees. He turned away from the dugout as men began filling in the hole, interring any bodies therein. The men looked like ants making due after an unseen force had disturbed their nest. Shells were still falling all around. A messenger came up to Kowalski.

"The company commander wants all platoon and section leaders to report to him at his bunker immediately," he said. Kowalski looked at Lange and then around him at seven helmeted heads who stared back at him. He wondered why he was the focus of their attention.

"Remember?" asked Lange. "That's you. You're the section leader." Kowalski grimaced and drudged off to the lieutenant's bunker.

"Orders have just arrived," Pfeiffer began looking over the faces of his soldiers in the candle lit bunker. He had commanded for only a month. When he had arrived he had taken special care to place a face with a name. It was one of his management tricks. He had found out very early that men worked harder if they were given recognition by name occasionally. Even a reprimand was taken with much less resistance if a manager scolded by using a man's Christian name. But this job was different. Four weeks ago there were more names and faces. Now, those that were left were indistinguishable from any other men. Their names had faded from his memory as their uniforms became covered in mud and their faces took on a haggard chalky color. They all looked alike now. He wondered what he looked like to them. "We have been ordered to recover the positions we have just lost." There was an audible groan. Pfeiffer ignored it. He was glad Kluggmann had been evacuated. That man would have found words to express the moan. "The preparation bombardment will begin at 0130 and continue for five minutes. We will attack at 0135."

"What of our flanks?" asked someone in the audience.

"The Bavarians have also been ordered to retake their lost ground so they will be on our flank." There were a few grunts to that statement. Pfeiffer countered the disbelief by placing a sense of urgency in his voice. It was another of his tricks to get compliance. He began speaking in short, brisk statements; no fancy elaborate instructions. "This is an all out attack. There is no plan. Just reoccupy the area we have just left and hold it. We will not advance on the French position once we have regained ours. Consolidate and prepare to repel the counterattack. I will blow my whistle at 0135. Get everyone out and forward. Two machine guns will give us cover fire for a time. Have your men pick up grenades and extra ammunition." Pfeiffer checked his watch. "Dismissed!" The terse statements had had their effect. No one hovered near to ask questions or offer comments after everyone was out of the way. Pfeiffer congratulated himself.

Lange sat on the fire step. He fidgeted. He stood. He paced. He sat down again. His eyes always looked in the direction of Pfeiffer's bunker. After a few moments he repeated all the movements. Two of the no-name soldiers talked and pointed at Lange. A third one made a low laugh sound but caught it up when Lange looked at him menacingly. Lange wondered which one would die first. A sly smirk crossed his lips. The no-name soldiers' shoulders sagged and a look of distress registered in their eyes. Each had questioned himself about being safe with the Old Folks even though one had fallen to wounds. They wondered if Lange was the good luck succubus. Could he have become the strongest of the drinkers of good luck? Had he taken Kluggmann's luck? Would he turn on them? Finally Kowalski came around the traverse. Lange sprang to his feet and swiftly walked to him smiling.

"What's up? Has there been any news of Kluggmann?" Lange asked.

"Counterattack." A pause. "No news of Kluggmann and I doubt we'll get any." He stiffened his back to prepare himself to give commands. He remembered that a stiff back always gave people an air of authority. He pointed at one of the no-names. "You, get grenades and give each man three." He pointed at another soldier. "You, get extra ammunition. One bandolier for each man. Anyone got a watch?" Lange raised his hand slowly, an innate gesture from his interrupted school days. Kowalski's voice was confusing him. Shouldn't they be smoking cigarettes and cajoling one another about their losses. Kluggmann. Liebermann. Both gone in the blink of an eye. Never to be seen again. Was it too much to ask to receive a warm word or a silent, sympathetic gesture? The philosopher seemed to have died also but there were no wounds. Was he the only unchanged one? "The bombardment will start at 0130 and the attack will begin when it stops five minutes later. The lieutenant will blow his whistle when it is time to attack. Everyone goes forward to recapture what we lost earlier tonight. Go no further. Once we are back in our trenches we defend them."

"But what about over there?" Lange pointed to where the French had flanked them.

"The Bavarians have been ordered to reclaim what they lost also. They will attack at the same time."

At Verdun cannon bombardments never stopped. They slackened on occasion but they never completely stopped. The amount of shells that fell on opposing lines could not be calculated. As a result, recognizing when a specific bombardment was begun, its duration, and whether or not it had stopped was indistinguishable to those who were in the melee. Nor could a soldier determine who was bombarding him. French and German rounds fell on the same areas at the same time. What a soldier could say at any given time was that a particular bombardment's rate of explosions was increasing or decreasing. Such was the case at 0130. The German artillery increased its rate of fire on a particular section on the west bank of the Meuse. Six batteries were dedicated to the bombardment. The loaders and gunners worked in unison. One shoved the shell into the breach. One closed the breach and another pulled the cord which sent the shell on its way. Well coordinated crews were so precise in their routine that a new shell was loaded at the recoil of the one being fired so that I seemed that the gun took on what was later to be called automatic fire. Stripped to the waist in even the coldest weather the loaders sweated rivers shoving one round after the other into the breach. For five minutes twenty-four guns spat ten rounds a minute. Sights were adjusted every ten rounds to make sure the deadly rain fell on the enemy and not friends; however, at that speed of reloading no one could be sure where the rounds were actually landing. Artillery observers phoned in sighting corrections when the phones were working but as one side's fire rate increased so did the other side's rate increase. Telephone lines were among the first casualties which left communication to runners. The runners had to pass through the bombardment to reach the batteries. Too often, the runner never reached the guns and as a result the batteries continued to fire on the same spot until stop or redirection orders were received. Many a soldier was grateful for their artillery's support in a fight and equally as grateful when the firing stopped.

The artillery's rate of fire increased until it resembled one vast explosion. Single shell detonations were undistinguishable. For five minutes the noise was more than deafening. The noise made ears ring as if they were in a bell tower while some ears slowly went deaf as they oozed blood. Communications between humans was done with sign language. Winds from the explosions beat the soldiers' faces and furled their clothing. Once rosy cheeks took on an ashy color and grey faces became a burnt red. Dirt mixed with the acrid air and made it almost unbreathable. A few soldiers fell in spasms pierced by red hot shrapnel or chewed up by high explosive shell splinters. 0130 came and went and 0135 seemed to be borne by the legs of a turtle. Men trembled at the thought of leaving the shelter of the fallen trees. Some sobbed ever so quietly. Others stared into the sky in an attempt to see the shells in their flight. Those who wished to survive pressed themselves against the trench walls or on to the ground at the bottom of a newly formed shell crater. Under such devastation a soldier felt helpless. He entered into a cycle of emotions. The helpless feeling gave way to anger; an anger that consumed every thought and controlled every movement. Anger turned to frustration over not being in control of oneself. Then, after only a few moments, the frustration turned back into helplessness and then anger again. For the inexperienced the cycle soon led to acceptance; an acceptance that the sounds they were hearing were going to be their last memory. Lange, a veteran of more months than the no-names, took relieve in knowing that in five minutes he would again be master of his own fate as he left the protection of the earth and ran forward to do battle. Hand to hand combat, as bloody and personal as it was, was a release. Out there among the bayonet thrusts, flying fists and pistol shots that was where acceptance of one's fate had meaning.

A whistle blew but went unheard. Pfeiffer recognized the fault. The artillery was too loud. He poked the man next to him in the ribs motioning with his head and hands to pass on the poke and charge. That was another mistake. Poking and motioning each man would take time. The men would enter the fight as individuals and not as a group in which men had more courage. 'Damn the sharpshooters,' he said to himself. He didn't care if they saw that he was the leader. He was angry with himself that he had not seen the mistakes in his instructions. The anger made him feel the invulnerability of youth. He jumped up on the parapet and frantically waived his hands about and blew hard on the whistle. A very forceful blow propelled the whistle out of his mouth and into the darkness. Flares arced into the night.

"C'mon, men. Forward!" He saw that men's mouths were open.

No sound came from them yet Pfeiffer knew that they were shouting. Yes. Yes. Encourage one another with senseless shouting. No slogans. Just a deep throated bellow. Strangely, the exploding shells kept anyone from hearing it. Only the man who shouted knew of its important.

The artillery slowed in the attack area but increased behind it. In the fading light of a star shell Pfeiffer assessed how many men had gotten out of the strong point then he turned to join those who were in the lead. He saw only the ones in front noting those who fell but regained their feet and continued on. A few did not get up but instead writhed in what appeared to be pain. People never died instantly unless an artillery shell's fragment ripped them in two. A bullet or multiple bullets entering the body didn't always kill outright. There was always a moment or two before death in which the wounded man felt what looked like dreadful pain. Few had the good fortune to get a painless death.

Pfeiffer waved his hands again. In the feeble light he saw more men come out of the trench. Shrapnel shells burst overhead. The explosion propelled bullets thudded all around. Some men screamed or was it a passing shell? Machine gun bullets flew high above. Pfeiffer turned and ran toward the objective catching up with the first men who had left the trench. He took what appeared to be the lead. He called over this shoulder goading them on through his example, if they were aware of his existence. Dirt infested air went down his throat and he coughed but did not slacken his pace. How many men followed him he wondered? It was too late for worrying about that yet he tried some math. He had had fifty with him in the strong point and twelve had returned from the other half company. How many was that he asked himself but the answer eluded him. Something inside his head was pounding. The steady thump-thump jerked his muscles involuntarily. He realized that he was trembling even though he didn't have fear. 'Control. Control,' he told himself.

He became oblivious to anyone's existence except his own. His once encouraging words became gasps that no one understood or tried to. He tripped on some protruding barb wire but kept himself from falling with a well placed hand. The wire's barb pierced his hand and brought an awareness of his surroundings back to crystal clarity.

Three or four soldiers were steering their runs toward him. 'Why did some men feel safety in running with the officers?' Pfeiffer screamed inwards. "Leave me alone!" he shouted at them but the din of the explosions drowned him out. The men smiled at him, a frightened, sickly smile, as they drew nearer, their steps equaling his pace. The soldiers had interpreted his unheard words as encouragement to accompany him. Inwardly he scolded them. 'Didn't they understand that officers were as frail as they were? They died in the same manners as any other soldier. I can no more protect you than I can protect myself.'

Kowalski nudged Lange and Lange nudged a no-name. They were all on the parapet and then running forward. No one shot his rifle. There was nothing to shoot at. Where was the enemy everyone was asking? Many eyes squinted to see an enemy that wasn't there. Many questioned if the foe was really there. Star shells burst. Machine gun bullet became Valkyries filling the sky plucking out men's lives from their bodies. In the flares' lights the stars died. Some wondered if the clouds hid the stars or if the stars had simply gone out. Everyone was shouting to encourage himself, no one else could hear the insane cries. Thud. Thud. Two soldiers were propelled backwards from the force of the bullets that had invaded their bodies. The shock on their faces was a classic work of astonishment and remorse. Lange fell forward scraping his nose. He fumbled himself upright sliding on the mud. He was more concerned about breaking a leg than receiving a bullet to the brain. A broken leg, if not set fast enough, could become infected and the surgeons took great relish in cutting off the appendage rather than trying to cure it. His mind was the home of a thousand angry bees. He wanted relief from the buzzing and the sting of mental pain they caused.

Kowalski turned to see how many were following. He counted to seven but some from other platoons were mixing in with his men. No matter. Strength in numbers. In the second it took to make a quick estimation, two fell and did not get up. Kowalski looked for Lange. To his benefit, Lange's small stature allowed him to become invisible on the battle field. Tall people, like Kowalski, always stood out as targets. Kowalski crouched in his run. Try to be smaller than Lange, he told himself.

Pfeiffer fell into one of the old communications trenches and for a moment allowed himself to catch his breath. 'You cannot stay here,' he told himself. 'Those men who are following you will think you have been hit and will abandon the attack. Some would even come looking for him. They wanted to be heroes and there was nothing more heroic as saving an officer. With the feat came a piece of ribbon that a soldier could display on his chest to his grandchildren. The grandchildren would never know that such a heroic sacrifice also spared the man who accompanied the wounded officer out of the battle and on to the dressing station.' Pfeiffer climbed out of the trench and waived his arms around to show that he was unhurt and also to gather the men. He pointed in the direction he thought they should go but he was unsure. Bullets whizzed by him or caught at his coat. A falling man collided with the lieutenant. The soldier's arms wrapped themselves around Pfeiffer's legs causing him to fall. As he cascaded to the ground the man's rifle butt hit the lieutenant in the head. The jolt caused a moment of unconsciousness. When he became aware again, Pfeiffer opened his eyes and looked on the face of a dead man.

'Who are you?' Pfeiffer asked the corpse without speaking. He looked at the lifeless eyes and wondered if there was rest in death. He wrestled his body erect again and began to run. Without thinking, he drew his pistol and deliberately cocked it ejecting an unspent bullet and chambering another. The motion of charging the pistol gave him a new confidence that propelled him forward into a frantic run.

Shells burst all around. Kowalski and Brach fell into a trench and recognized it as their old position. They had made it. Instinctively, each tossed a hand grenade over the flanking traverses. Consideration was not given to the fact that friendly soldiers may have been in the area. The lack of screams or returning grenades led them to the decision that they had arrived first and there were no poilus to fight. A few more soldiers fell into the trench and aimed their rifles at Kowalski and Brach. One of them shot but missed. Brach kicked him and was about to bayonet him when he realized he was one of his own men. Kowalski laughed. He saw the meeting as unbelievably funny. Brach thumped Kowalski's helmet with his rifle butt. The laughing faded into a confused face. It was as if he had woken from a dream. Where had the last minutes gone?

Kowalski forced his way past newly arrived soldiers and ran to where he remembered the dugouts to be. In each he tossed a grenade. There were no screams of death, just hollow echoes. Pfeiffer fell into the trench almost on top of Kowalski. Everything was funny again but Kowalski stifled a laugh as he bent over to help the lieutenant up; however, the smile did not leave his face. Pfeiffer saw the upturned corners of Kowalski's mouth and became confused. Any kind of humor seemed so out of place among the carnage that its appearance seemed a paradox to the point of madness. Kowalski broke the confusion when he realized who he had in his hands. He stiffened and reported.

"I have the duty and pleasure to report that there are no enemies in this position."

"Have you searched the dugouts?"

"With grenades, Herr Lieutenant. Brach is that way." He pointed. Pfeiffer turned and began running along the trench looking into the faces of those he met and placing them in a defensive posture against the parapet. He stopped at one man and looked critically at him. Through the layers of mud, he made out the Adrienne helmet of a poilu.

"Here. This man isn't one of ours. Make him a prisoner." Everyone looked at the man in astonishment. The poilu looked at them with the same surprise mirrored on his face. The dream snapped shut. The Frenchman threw done his rifle and unbuckled his equipment in one fluid movement. His hands went over his head. Two soldiers took the poilu to a dugout that would act as his prison until they had time to take him to the back area.

"It appears that they drove us out but they didn't occupy it," Brach told Pfeiffer. The shells were still bursting. Pfeiffer took out his notebook scribbled a note and gave it to a soldier telling him to deliver it to battalion. The man looked at the exploding shells, listened to squealing bullets, and watched arcing flares. Without thought he grabbed the note and ran. He had no idea where battalion was or even a safe direction to run in. He just ran.

More men were arriving. Brach placed them in position to repel a counterattack. He thanked his lucky, unseen stars that the French had not reversed the trench walls. That would have been exhausting work to reset. Some men had lost their rifles. He sent a man to retrieve weapons and ammunition from the fallen cautioning the man not to stop for any wounded.

"Tell them where we are and that they should make their way here." Brach reasoned that the stronger ones who made it to the trench would have less critical wounds. They could be used in defense. Those who couldn't make it were of use only to the doctors who practiced surgery. They would not be of any use in defense. Dying in the muck would be better than dying on the operating table full of hope of survival. Pfeiffer appeared again and shook Brach's hand. Both were pleased with themselves and their success.

They grinned from ear to ear as if they had stolen the hot pie from the farmer's wife's window sill. Now they must hold until they were relieved. The noise was lessening.

"How many have we?" asked Pfeiffer.

"I'll go and count," answered Braun. Pfeiffer moved along the trench to find Kowalski and asked him the same question. Kowalski shrugged but turned to go and find out. Pfeiffer saw Lange and motioned him come over to him. Before Lange could reach Pfeiffer, the lieutenant was on his knees clutching his head. It appeared that the lieutenant had been hit. Lange grabbed at Pfeiffer and called out.

"Help me here," Lange shouted at a no-name. Lange and the soldier sat Pfeiffer down with his back to the trench wall. Lange stared in dismay at the hole in the top of Pfeiffer's helmet. A piece of shrapnel had neatly pierced it. He ripped Pfeiffer's helmet off and was greeted by a stream of blood. He pulled a handkerchief from his pocket and slapped it on where he thought the wound was to stifle the blood flow. The no-name tore open a first aid package and added the pad to the handkerchief. The blood stopped. Perplexed by the rapidity of the blood stopping, Lange chanced a look under the two dressings. To his amazement he found a shallow wound. Skin broken but the projectile had not entered the skull.

Pfeiffer gasped as a man just rescued from drowning. His hand jerked instinctively to where he felt pain. He felt under the dressing Lange had applied expecting to slid a finger into a hole. There was wetness but not a gaping hole. He opened his eyes and attempted to talk but could not find the breath. He gasped, panted, coughed, and spat. Sometimes ridiculous thoughts come to the mind of those who feel that they are approaching death. Pfeiffer inwardly asked himself if he had eaten before the attack. The answer had everything to do with dignity. He had seen many men hit who defiled themselves by vomiting their last meal over themselves and those who were trying to help. He had viewed those people with disgust and horror and had hoped he would not end up the same way. Through the tears that had welled up in response to the pain Pfeiffer managed words.

"Where am I hit?"

"There's a slight wound on top of your head but nothing more!"

"But something knocked me down." Pfeiffer struggled to his knees with Lange's help. The men he had put in guard positions were starting to cluster around him. The lieutenant sensed that they were taking away his air, the air he needed to survive just a little longer. Frantically, he screamed at them. "Get back to your posts!" Lange was shocked and withdrew his support of the lieutenant. Pfeiffer lurched forward almost falling. "Not you," he said to Lange. "Help me to my feet." Lange thrust his shoulder into the lieutenant's side and pushed him toward the trench wall where he steadied himself and rose. He winced as pain shot through his head but he stood. Lange handed him his helmet which clanged. Pfeiffer looked into the helmet to find the shrapnel ball that had hit him lodged in one of the liner pillows. The helmet had slowed the spent round enough to avert death. Lange smiled when he saw the bullet.

"That's twice in as many hours that a person was near death and survived. We're a lucky bunch," observed Lange. "I hope the luck runs in threes and I'm next. Anyone who survives such near misses will survive the war and lead a charmed life after it's over." The lieutenant put the bullet in his pocket and put his helmet back on keeping the double bandage still in place. The weight of his steel helmet increased the pain but only momentarily.

"Counterattack coming!" yelled a soldier. The lieutenant, the pain exorcised from his mind, ran to the man and asked where. The soldier pointed. Kowalski came up and gave the lieutenant a flare pistol. He pointed it in the air and fired. In a few seconds the flare exploded bathing the landscape in a white light. The sight was brief but there they were, Poilus running at them. Pfeiffer selected a red flare and shot it into the air. As soon as it exploded machine gun bullets flew through the air. Pfeiffer and his men ducked below ground level as the bullets flew overhead just skimming the parados. One of the no-name soldiers started activating grenades and throwing them over the parapet without looking. Lange joined him. The soldiers passed grenades to the two throwers. Each threw with all his might until their arms ached and he had to stand down. Another soldier immediately took his place and continued throwing. The machine guns stopped and Kowalski chanced a look. He could see only the blackness. Pfeiffer sent up a white flare and Kowalski tried again to see. The brilliant light revealed a barren unpopulated landscape. Bodies were strewn everywhere. Some writhed in pain while others appeared to be deflated balloons dressed in muddy rags. The counterattack had been broken. Pfeiffer scribbled a note, selected a man and told him to report that the lost ground had been recovered. The note also asked to be relieved at once by a stronger force that could retain the ground. If the French attacked again in even half company strength, his garrison would be overwhelmed.

As the runner left Brach reported that he had counted thirty men, four of which had no weapons. Kowalski reported that all seven of his platoon had survived. Relief could not arrive too soon. In one day, Pfeiffer's company had gone from one hundred fifty men to thirty-seven. 'How many will I have left by the time the relief comes?' Pfeiffer wondered. He turned to Brach.

"Place five men on watch evenly spaced and let the others sleep. But don't let them take off their equipment or start any fires. We will be relieved soon. I'll reestablish company headquarters in our old dugout or the closest one to it. Make your report on defenses to me in ten minutes." Braun turned to carry out the instructions as Pfeiffer went to find the old company command post. After orienting himself he took a few paces and pushed aside a heavy drape. On the other side was a roofless hole. He moved on to the next dugout which had a partial roof. Pfeiffer picked up some of the roof's bigger pieces that had fallen into the dugout and attempted to finish the roof. He managed a cover of corrugated iron pieces and a waterproof sheet. The rain began to fall. The sheet sagged as it accumulated water. Pfeiffer knew that the sheet would eventually give way but in the mean time he used it to his advantage. He poked a hole in it and the water streamed out and into his water bottle. When the bottle was full, he opened his mouth to the flow and allowed the excess to wash over his face. The cold water overflowing his mouth refreshed him and soaked his uniform's front. The water soaked through to his chest. For a few minutes, the coolness was heaven itself and then it became bothersome as it washed down into his trousers. He went outside and stretched the sheet more tautly across the roof weighting it down with heavy lumber. Inside, the hole still leaked but the sheet no longer sagged. He brought out and lit a candle sticking it in a bottle that sat on a grocer's box. He paused and read the label that had not completely come off. Peaches. What he wouldn't do to have that box still full of cans. Brach stuck his head in the dugout.

"There you are." Pfeiffer nodded and plopped down on the muddy floor. There was room only for three in the dugout and they had to be crouched down because of the low ceiling. "The men are hungry as usual but they are wide awake. The artillery is continuing and since I last reported two men have been wounded. One serious while the other is more whines than injury. The French are no where in sight. There is shooting in the direction of the Bavarians. Should I send someone over to find out how that is going?" Pfeiffer nodded.

"Send Lange. He knows the way." Brach left. Pfeiffer took his helmet off and risked taking the bandage off. Slowly he lifted the mass and felt where he thought the wound would be. His fingertips felt through the gore of dried blood to find a slight gash. It still oozed some blood but that was normal for a head wound. He replaced the bandage with one from his own medical pack. As an afterthought he reached in his pocket and brought out the offending bullet to marvel at it. He inspected it for some markings but there were none. He threw it in the air, caught it and put it back in his pocket. He promised himself that when he was in the rest area he would have a hole drilled in it and a cord strung threw it. The round was his good luck charm. It would hang around his neck for ever after. He allowed himself to drift off to sleep.

Chapter 10
Reunion

Remembrance. The occasion was the funeral of President Paul von Hindenburg, once Field Marshal of the Imperial German Army. Chancellor Adolf Hitler had made an appeal to all those who had served with the Field Marshal to come to the battle memorial at Tannenberg in East Prussia to form an honor guard. He had encouraged the veterans to wear their old uniforms that gathered dust in trunks and attics serving as buffets for moths. The chancellor's reason for such a grand send off was not lost on the people. It was a farewell to the old order and a salute to the new society that he envisioned for Germany. Peter Lange saw his attendance at the funeral as his duty to the old order, the system which had robbed him of his youth and forced him into a radically different post war world that he had no part in forming. He would bear witness to the internment of his lost life. However, he would not bear witness to the birth of a new German Reich. As soon as the funeral was over, he and his wife would leave for a new start in Australia.

Lange stood at attention in his old Imperial uniform in front of the full length mirror in the parlor of his modest Berlin apartment. A faint smell of naphtha hung about him in a cloud. There was a feeling of snugness here and there but on the whole, the uniform of sixteen years ago fit him well. His wife had told him so. He stood looking at himself from all the angles to make sure his frau had not just been kind in her opinion. In that reflected image, Lange had to admit that he did cut a very military figure even though his furrowed face and greyed hair betrayed his age. He found that it was easy to envision himself as the youth of 1915. He managed to stand up even taller, straightening his back. The greyness of the uniform gave the impression that he was clad in medieval armor. Once again he was a knightly volunteer filled with the desire to defend his country against all comers. His back muscles rebelled against the erect posture and he slumped forward a little and back to the image in the apartment mirror. An involuntary smile crossed his lips as he reprimanded himself. He must think of himself in the real world and not in the past. 'You only looked this good when they gave you the first uniform,' he told himself, 'or on parade for some visiting general who said he sympathized with the soldier's blight and wanted to go home also.' Then he saw himself as the disillusioned soldier of 1916 at Verdun. The uniform was mud covered, tattered and spattered with the blood of opponents and comrades. He was indistinguishable as a soldier. Finally, he saw the newly made officer flush with pride who commanded the Stosstruppen in the final battle on the Somme his automatic pistol pointed at the hundreds of British prisoners who threw up their hands in surrender. Involuntarily he reached up and brushed the dust from his shoulder boards. He straightened his back again despite the bodily complaints and remembered the final assault across the Marne that had promised to break the trench line. His hand went to his chest where the bullet holes had been. There had been two neat ones. One had been deflected by a package in his pocket but the other had shattered a rib and torn away part of his shoulder blade as it left. On this uniform, given to him as he left hospital after a painful recovery, the holes had never existed. With the same hand he felt for the small packet that had probably saved his life although none of the pain that he had had to endure. It had been his final letter and those few personal articles that he had cautioned many comrades to send to his home after his death. For some odd reason he had never entrusted it with anyone after Kluggmann had been wounded. He panicked when he didn't find the lump that it had always produced. Then he remembered; destroyed when he was wounded. It was so blood soaked that the orderlies had thrown it away along with his uniform.

As the images faded, Lange asked his great philosophical question. Was there any remorse over his actions? Verdun. The Somme. The Marne. The first battle, Verdun, had been the one of the armies in which they fought to defend the country. There was valor in that fight. Humility. Honor. People at home watched that struggle in the newspapers. The headlines had screamed of the army's great advances and that the enemy was on the verge of capitulating. All that was needed was one more effort. The people marveled at how bravely their husbands, sons, relatives fought and they commented on how this or that thrust against the enemy was surely the crippling blow. For those whose kin did not fall, the struggle was cheered and toasted with bitter beer. There were no celebrations for those who fell. Lange had read the newspapers that managed to get to the trenches and had been gratified that someone somewhere was winning the battles. It was not he.

The second battle, the Somme, had been a battle of movement. His Stosstruppen detachment of twenty-five men had catapulted itself out of the world of trenches and into the fields that lay beyond. They had come to grips with the once unseen enemy hurdling grenades and firing into their faces when they resisted. The battle was exhilarating after the months of troglodyte existence. Downtrodden men surrendered to him even though he was armed with only a pistol and sometimes that pistol hadn't any ammunition in it. But the joie de vivre soon gave way to exhaustion as the commanders pushed the stormtroopers on and on. His twenty-five men group dwindled to five in the space of seven days. When the halt was finally called; there was nothing left to give. He and his men existed between reality and another-worldliness. They were numb with fatigue and inured to death in a macabre way. He had come to envision heaps of corpses, badly mutilated bodies, as part of the French landscape. A pile of humanity here or there was not uncommon or was the stink that came from them. The only remorse he felt was when he came upon the bodies of horses or dogs. They had died without a cause.

The final battle, the Marne, was one of daily survival. The actual enemy was rarely seen. Instead, there were powerful almost supernatural forces to contend with in the exploding artillery shells, streams of machine gun bullets, and the ever present but invisible sharpshooters who ended lives one bullet at a time. Lange had not been able to raise his weapon and fire at these dealers in death. They were bodiless spirits that plucked men from the world like Valkyries lifting men's souls from the field to take them to Valhalla. In that battle Lange became an unfeeling animal who strove to satisfy his need for food and water. He trained the men under his command to fight for those two things above all else. Gone were the causes of defense and rapid movement to reach an objective. Lange taught them how life meant nothing on the battle field. One survived only through food and water. His men soon understood what he meant. They became as careless as he in seeking these two coveted rewards. They volunteered for the rear guard where they could pillage the supply dumps left behind by the retreat back to Germany. When the enemy showed itself he and his men grabbed what they could and melted away. They never fired a shot. Detachment 16 became a synonym for bravery in the minds of the divisional and corps commanders. They were mentioned in dispatches and given boxes of medals. But in reality they were only making sure they had enough to eat and drink until the end finally came. He felt his heart racing; the adrenalin flowed through his blood stream, drums pounded in his head. The noise of artillery shells exploding deafened him and machine gun bullets whizzed around him. Over the din he heard a voice. It was the voice of safety; a feminine voice that brought him back out of the haze to once again admire himself.

"Haven't you been listening to me, Esel?" she asked looking concerned. Tonya had seen that far away look often over the years since they married in 1920. Sometimes her Peter would go months without that look but eventually something would trigger it to return. In the middle of the night, she would find him lying on his back; wide awake, his eyes vacant, staring at the ceiling and sweating. He would sweat even in the coldest of nights. The first few times she had panicked and ran down the apartment building's corridor calling for the porter to fetch the doctor. After the fourth such panic the doctor stopped coming. He had assured her from the beginning that there was nothing he could do and that he had seen the same symptoms in many men. He sympathetically told her that she should count her lucky stars that Peter had not turned to alcohol or drugs to deal with the attacks as others had done or to disappearing all together. Eventually, she learned to simply watch him, to soothe him with comforting words in the darkness of their bedroom. His face never changed and she felt that her efforts were in vain but in a few moments his eyes closed and he snored. In the years that followed, the paralyzed, unseeing and unhearing episodes passed. Instead, he would get out of bed and go to sit at the kitchen table looking into the darkness with saddened eyes sipping on a cup of vile coffee laced with English rum. Her husband was off fighting the war again, she would say to herself but, nevertheless, remain awake until he returned to bed.

Tonya had tried to keep him away from the thoughts that stimulated the memories but they flooded back at the most inopportune times, before dinner when the smells of food flooded the apartment or as he looked out of the windows into falling rain. He may not have disappeared into humanity as so many others had but, because of those bouts, he had withdrawn from social life. He was well liked by those he worked with but they knew they were not his friends. He had no friends among the living only among those he called the Old Folks. He was hospitable toward her family; his own family had been his mother who had died before the war had ended. Nevertheless, there were occasions when Peter had momentarily disappeared, never months or days, just a few hours.

Germans are a punctual people. Daily activities seem to take on a schedule. They left work at a certain time, give or take only a few minutes. They arrived home at the same time Monday through Saturday. And they sat down to eat an evening meal precisely at the same time as the day before and the day before that. Shortly after they were married Peter failed to walk through the door at the prescribed hour. Tonya waited wringing her hands in nervousness at the kitchen table as minutes stretched into hours. She had tried to keep calm reasoning that there could be many causes for his delay. A traffic jam. The tram may have broken down. Maybe an old friend had asked him to a drink. After three hours she bundled herself into her shawl and went searching too embarrassed to ask anyone for help. She had to accomplish it by herself. The park near his office was the first place she looked. She found him there sitting on a bench staring at the street lamp. Silently she sat next to him and took his hand in hers. His hand had been so cold. He turned his face to her and he looked through her for a few seconds with cold eyes. Then, as if the sun had just risen to melt the night's thin ice, he saw her for who she was. 'Hello', he would say and squeeze her hand. 'Haven't I met you somewhere before? You had better go away before my wife comes to collect me.' Or he would say something about how her reputation would be sullied with a man like him. They would laugh then rise from the bench and walk home. Other times she found him on the tram that he would have normally taken home staring into nothingness or fast asleep. The bus conductor, an occupational friend, had come to know Peter over the years. He would not disturb him when he lapsed into those states. He had seen that type of behavior before in others and respected it. The driver also knew that Peter's wife would soon track him down. He was used to seeing the well-dressed slender woman with the pale blue eyes gently sit beside Peter take his hand and say something in a low, comforting voice. The driver never heard the words but the calm composure that Tonya displayed even made him relax. Peter would noisily inhale as if he were tasting air for the first time and then his face took on the demeanor of a child just waking from a nap. He would look about him and ask, without mouthing the words, where he was. Then he would greet Tonya with a gentle hello. She would reply, no words. He would become confused and stammer a few words while looking deeply into her eyes. Then there would be a gush of words. Excuses for why he was where he was. Tonya would listen attentively all the way home. Often they rode the tram twice around its route. As they got off the tram, she would always reprimand the conductor for this or that with a wink and the conductor would apologize with a smile and a nod agreeing to be more attentive towards his customers. The walk home was in silence. These incidents had become less frequent over the years until finally they had ceased altogether. Yet Tonya feared that they might occur again at any time. It was not a demeanor she had expected from a soldier.

When they had met and married Tonya, like so many who grew up during the war, had envisioned Peter as a romantic, tragic hero. She fantasized that he had been one of Dumas's Three Musketeers when she looked at the studio portraits of her husband in uniform that his mother had commissioned when he was on furlough. He appeared so resolute, earnest. Her girlish mind saw him standing on the ramparts defying thousands of bullets, brandishing his sword at the enemy and swearing oaths that would make sailors turn green with envy. She was sure that less heroic men gathered to his leadership and cheered him to feats beyond bravery while they followed him into the fires of hell. She even fanaticized that he had been impervious to any harm the foe could throw at him and he had returned from battles covered in laurels from both sides engaged in the conflict. After a time, those visions faded aided by stories Peter would tell her when the lamp light burned low and the mealtime wine had mellowed him. In those stories she saw her husband become a figure not unlike a mud covered caveman, hiding in holes, and grubbing for food and water. He told her of his comrades and how different yet alike he was to them. The story of being wounded had shocked her. Slowly she began to understand how he was a hero only because he had survived the war. She had predicted that putting on his ancient uniform would bring about an episode and tried to discourage him from wearing it. He had remained obstinate about being properly dressed for the occasion and she had finally demurred.

"I was remembering how I was so filled with romanticism at the beginning. How I had seen myself as the savior of the nation," Lange answered her question. "My god, how skinny I was and barely old enough to shave." He laughed and turned to her to lightly kiss her forehead. She giggled in a childish way that never ceased to make him smile even in the worst time. It was the only sound, that of a child, he was without.

Tonya was both grateful and despondent about having no children. Grateful because she felt that he would have been inattentive in raising them and despondent because she was sure the children would have had a calming effect on those frayed nerves. In a voice filled with bravado he said, "You know I wasn't in the least bit afraid when the shells started bursting and the men started dying." She nodded. She had heard that before and wondered each time if he really meant it or if he was lying to himself. Lange could see the doubt on her face when he launched into these attempts to describe himself to her. She was a good wife but dispelling the school taught images of the iron men at the front had been hard for him.

Lange kept himself from telling a story, turned to the mirror again and smoothed the seams of his uniform. Tonya giggled again leaving him to his mirror. She took refuge in her kitchen fortress where she kept her world from crumbling too much. He did not pursue her into that realm. Instead he still stood before the mirror admiring himself. Memories of dead or mutilated comrades came and went and then he began wondering what had happened to the many types of vermin that had lived in his uniform; fleas, lice, and various other types of pests who had happy homes among the stitches. "I wonder who else will be at the funeral."

The site of the funeral was in East Prussia, a long train ride to the east. Lange had debated with himself about wearing the uniform on the train or changing to it after the ride. In the end his wife, still very afraid that the uniform would cause a mental incident, had convinced him to leave the uniform in his suitcase until he arrived at his destination. She feared that if he had an incident on the train no one would know what to do but at the funeral there would be many just like him who could help. As a compromise she told him that he could wear his Stosstruppen half boots with the puttees during the trip. Tonya accompanied him to the depot talking about how he should behave and to be sure to eat correctly. Lange listened with half a mind. The other half took stock of his future train mates. Some were dressed in their uniforms which made him regret having agreed to wear only his foot wear. Boarding was called for. Lange gently kissed Tonya. A tear betrayed her feelings.

"It's not like I'm going off to war," he said in a half scolding tone. "I'll be back in two days."

"It's just that we have never been apart since we married. The apartment will be so empty without the sound of you passing gas or knocking about in the kitchen over the complicated task of making tea." He laughed. A deep laugh. She looked offended but managed a smile. The tear dried and there were no more. He boarded said good-bye again from the car steps and the train started to move as if on cue of his words. Tonya followed the movement until the speed outpaced her walk. She waved her handkerchief. He was already out of sight in the compartment. The wave was answered by someone else who had mistaken it for him.

Once the train had managed a good pace Lange left his compartment for the dining car with his suitcase. There he found some in Imperial uniforms and some in the new political party uniforms. They greeted him as one passenger might greet another at the start of a journey. He glided through the small crowd without difficulty. Some noticed his boots and puttees but made no comment. Many dressed their legs that way in preparation for a field outing. His destination was the lavatory where he changed into his war togs. The atmosphere in the dining car changed when he emerged. He was greeted by applause and hurrahs. Those in uniform clapped him on the back and asked where he had fought. He shared hip flasks with many who had been at the same places as he although neither he nor they remembered each other. Other passengers in smart three piece suits rose to make a frenzied dash to the lavatory from which they too emerged in uniform and to cheers. Many bulged over their belts in their old uniforms but by standing perfectly erect some of the bulk disappeared. Tight collars were definitely a problem. Lange congratulated himself on his foresight to have the uniform tailored to his middle age physique. The population of the dining car grew as others responded to the growing noise that emanated from there. Its atmosphere changed from purposeful traveling businessmen to jubilant boasting soldiers who joked in loud voices that the government should have arranged for box cars to pick them up. Porters ran to and fro serving beer and other spirits. Soon someone organized a table clearing. Neatly stacked against the wall, the tables gave way to a spacious room in which everyone walked about freely engaging in groups. They all reminisced about the many rides they had endured in the forty men or eight horses cars. Lange kept his thoughts to himself and smiled as he mused about how conveniently they had forgotten about the discomfort of unheated cars in the winter and the smelly stifling wagons in the summer not to mention the cramped space they had endured on treks that went on for days without end. Then there were the lice that resided in every nook and cranny despite the disinfectant. Droves of them had dined on soldiers when they fell asleep on the bare floors. There was always a tale of some poor, hapless soul who had disappeared during a trip never to be seen again. The tale teller swore that an investigation had revealed that the vermin had wholly eaten him uniform and all.

The otherwise boring trip to East Prussia took on an atmosphere of revelry even though there was a funeral to attend at its terminus. Lange wrote down many names and addresses in his notebook and made an equal amount of promises to visit in the near future. When the train made stops, a few volunteered, jokingly, to go on ration detail. Everyone chipped in and the volunteers ran into the nearby village to purchase brandy, beer, and food. The dining car inventory reflected the times, depression limited the quantities of everything much in the same as the British blockade had done during the war. Stocks had run out within hours of rolling into the countryside. When the ration party returned, they were applauded and then the stories about being on the ration party details would begin. Most talked about the mud but few talked about the curtains of artillery fire or machine gun barrages they had to endure in securing food and water. All the tales included starlit nights in which the teller looked into the heavens and had thought up some philosophical observation which had served his as a motto from then on. There was no mention of comrades who were lost during those forays. Lange remembered his trip with Liebermann and pulling the soldier out of the mud with the tree branch. He avoided the memory of consigning Liebermann's body to the mud. As time went on, the merry making group grew smaller. A few of the veterans withdrew with their personal thoughts to their compartments where they covered themselves in a blanket and closed their eyes. But sleep was only feigned. Instead they relived the memories of paralyzing fears, fallen comrades, lost youth, and the blind anger that had possessed them when they felt so helpless under the weapons of the artillery gods. The copious amounts of liquor took another toll as aged men involuntarily dropped off to sleep in the dining car. They either failed to respond or ignored the prodding of the train attendants to clear the car in preparation of breakfast. These men had no fears of the past. The alcohol drowned out the emotion. Lange envied them their peace. As night grew deeper, the car grew as silent as it could. Only the varied snoring tones managed to disturb some. Too soon the smells of breakfast permeated the air. Those who had remained in the car now responded to urgings to leave. As the last managed to exit the conductor came through to announce that the train would arrive at the memorial near dawn. Lange sat at a window staring into the darkness that passed by at breakneck speed. Too many stories had stimulated too many emotions for him. Sleep was impossible but he was not in one of his trances. Tonya would be proud of how well he was handling the situation.

The train came to a halt in a wide pasture as blackness turned to gray in anticipation of a clear sunlit day. Stars' lights went out one after another until only the morning star was visible and then it blinked and was no more. The shimmering dew took the place of wonder. It blanketed the low plants leading the eye to believe a lake stretched itself off into the infinite distance. From his window Lange could see the Tannenberg Memorial. Its cold brick ramparts, fashioned on the ideal of a Teutonic fortress, stood on what appeared to be an island amid the moisture laden pasture. Limp banners were festooned to poles on each of the eight towers. He half expected to see mounted armored knights on the road to the memorial. Where had he seen such a sight before, he wondered?

The tranquility of the sleeping men was disturbed by young soldiers who burst into each passenger car as if borne by a cyclonic wind. There speech to the occupants was the same in each carriage. "Achtung. Achtung. Who is here for the funeral?" Bloodshot eyes rolled in dried sockets. A few were able to answer the question using intelligent words while some could only raise hands. The young soldiers tried to make a count but gave up as many rose to stretch or greet those they had spent the night drinking with. The young soldiers continued. "Funeral attendees are to get off here. I will lead you to your temporary quarters. Hurry, alte volk. The train must go on."

The old soldiers looked out the windows as Lange grabbed his valise and went to the door. One of the young folk stood next to him on the stairs and gave him a sidelong glance.

"You have kept yourself fit, Hauptman, not like some of these others. I can see that you were one of the ironman from my grandfather's stories."

Over the clattering of the car's wheels, Lange could hear the others complaining. Where was the station? Where were the bands of welcome? Some, still possessed of the spirited preceding day and night, thumped their chest and asked no one in particular whether they knew how important of a personage they were. Finally, the train rolled to a stop. Lange and the young person, a no-name, were the first to step on to firm ground. Both swayed a little in response to Newton's laws but recovered their composure quickly enough to satisfy young and old egos. Lange stood back to watch the others disembark. With their luggage in hand they gingerly jumped from the train to the ground, a distance of about a meter and a half. Someone joked that they may not have arrived in boxcars but the detraining was just as bad as it had been during the war. Lange remembered detraining during the war. Many had contrived to break an ankle or leg at those detrainings. Such an injury would take them to hospital while the others filed off to the killing fields. Now it was different. Some helped others get down. Others cautiously let themselves down fearing and complaining of the least little pains. The conductor and attendants had descended and offered help where it was needed. But there assistance was not altruistic. They merely expedited the clearing of the train. The young soldiers who had announced the train's arrival stood off as a group joking about this or that person who fell or stumbled. Lange was grateful that there were no crippled old soldiers among his group. Detraining would have been perilous for them. The thought almost froze Lange in his stride. 'Where are the invalids?' he asked himself. In answer he said, 'Maybe they were on another train that stopped where there was a platform.' Finally, after long minutes, the conductor remounted the car's platform and blew his whistle. The train gathered movement, the cars slipping by as if borne on a stream of water instead of steel rails. The people left in the cars glanced at the soldiers. None waved. None smiled. Children did not giggle.

Lange was surprised at the number of funeral participants. The car he had been in had regurgitated about fifty. A quick survey of the area showed about two hundred. Apparently other cars had also been full of ex-soldiers. The veterans mixed among themselves possibly to find comrades unseen since the war. There were a few reunions which were announced by bilious hellos and hands smacking other hands or backs. Lange looked for Kowalski and Kluggmann. He knew that Kowalski had survived the war but many years had passed since they had said good-bye first when Lange had received his commission and then again at demobilization when their paths

MICHAEL P. KIHNTOPF

had crossed purely by chance. As for Kluggmann, he had never returned to the platoon but his name had never appeared on the death
lists either. Lange assumed he had survived the evacuation and hospitals. Yet, there was doubt since deaths from wounds at German
civilian hospitals did not appear on regimental announcements.

"Please to come together," a young man shouted through a
megaphone. He was dressed in the new uniform of the Wehrmacht.
"Over that hill are your bivouac and other veterans who you might
know. There you will also receive instructions for tomorrow's funeral. Please let us clear the field. Other trains will be arriving shortly."
Grudgingly, the veterans moved in the direction indicated. Some
who had possibly been together during the war formed themselves
into marching groups. They jockeyed for position reminding one
another who marched where. There were more young soldiers on
the group's fringes who acted like sheep dogs in herding the old
ones along. No one was allowed to stray. It was a cool morning but
some still sweated and begged to be able to rest. The non-names
prodded them along. Some of the young smiled and talked while
others were disdainful and cold. Even though the chancellor was
a war survivor, he had fostered a concept of Germany belonging to
the youth and distanced himself from trappings of the old. Those
dour, youthful soldiers had undoubtedly succumbed to that reasoning, Lange thought. Nevertheless, their demeanor was impressive.
Straight backs, clear eyes and tailored uniforms. That was the image
of the new soldier. It was an image of a peacetime existence. Gone
was the mud, blood spattered uniforms and the faces of defeat that
had crossed the Rhine in November 1918. Lange wondered if he
should be prideful or critical. A man he had met the evening before
provided an answer.

"Don't those greyhounds look splendid? I see myself in them
when I volunteered. Full of vinegar and spoiling for a fight." He
slapped Lange on the back. "Remember? Ach, how it all came

tumbling down. Maybe they will avenge our defeat." Lange had neither agreed or disagreed but managed to ask, under his breath, who
these boys would fight against.

From the slight rise on to which the veterans were herded, Lange
saw below him row upon row of glistening bell tents. The morning
mists cleared off to show an almost picture perfect landscape surrounding the tent city. There were rolling hills among which sheep
and small cattle grazed on vermillion grass. Trees surrounded the
knolls. Their boughs gently swayed in the breezes as if they were
waving at the veterans. But was it a welcome or a shooing away?
Lange remembered the French forests that he and those around him
had pounded into matchwood. Was this forest fearful that these de-
spoilers had come to do them likewise? There was a winding broad
white roadway that led to the memorial's entrance. The encampment
where the veterans were to stay was to the left of the monument.
Seemingly, the canvas city stretched on for miles. The illusion was
caused by having each tent evenly spaced from one another on ruled
dirt walkways which ran up and out of sight over one of the many
rises. The ex-soldiers gasped their approval. Amid the tents field
gray clad soldiers, more veterans, wandered. When they saw the approaching mob, some attempted to go and greet them but the uniformed youths maintained their control and kept the mass moving
until it reached the center of the tent city. There, on a slightly raised
platform, stood an officer of the Sturmabteilung or SA , Hitler's
private army. Megaphone to his mouth, he gave instructions.

"Welcome to the funeral." His voice was of a high pitched tenor
tone. A few soldiers winced at its sound. Noises died away. The officer continued. "Please find your tent and drop off your luggage.
Each tent has a letter on it. You are to take a cot in the tent that
has the first letter of your last name. Once you have found the right
place, reform here for your morning meal and more instructions."
He put the megaphone down, stepped off the platform, and walked

into a tent on which the title of administration was displayed on a white board in black letters above the entrance. The mob streamed through the tents looking for the appropriate letter. Some shouted out the letters as they passed them in an effort to guide those who were still trying to catch their breath from the walk.

Tent found, Lange threw his grip at the first cot. He sat for a moment on the canvas bed and looked about. There were no other valises beside any of the beds. He asked himself if he should remain or find another tent that had some occupants. He decided not to make a decision until he had done a little more exploring. A shadow formed in the light that the open tent flap let in. It was one of the herders with a clip board.

"Your name?" he asked coldly.

"Peter Lange," Lange replied just as coldly purposely not rising to greet the stranger. The young man scanned the list on his clipboard. He found what he was looking for and came to attention.

"I beg your pardon for being so coarse just now, Herr Hauptman. I'm sure you understand that there are many who are not who they seem to be. They wear uniforms and insignias that are not theirs." Lange nodded. He had caught many a person in the dining car in a lie about their status and experiences but, as politeness would have it, did not call them out on the matter. Lange had reasoned that they should have their imaginary tale of bravado. Who would fault them but one of equal falsehood. The young soldier leafed through the many pages of paper that had been clipped beneath the name roster. Straightening up from the searching task he said, "I have two notes for you. One is from Army General Major Pfeiffer and the other is from SA Group Leader Kowalski." Lange almost broke into a laugh but squelched it when he saw how serious the youth was.

"No one has called me by my rank for many years," Lange said with an air of embarrassment to cover up the sound of amusement his voice could have betrayed. "I am no longer associated with the army." The no-name relaxed a little and feigned a smile that betrayed how close he still was to being a wide eyed child. But the familiarity died as quickly as it had surfaced when he handed over the envelopes that contained notes. The youth straightened even taller if that were possible, bowed slightly, and presented the envelopes with some well placed political advice.

"I would suggest visiting with Group Leader Kowalski before you meet with the army officer. It would show your political awareness." The youth turned and went to the next tent where he carried on with his duties. Lange ripped open Kowalski's note first.

Lange,

It will be so good to see you again. Go to the administration tent and tell the tent city mayor that you are to be sent to SA headquarters at once under orders from Group Leader Kowalski. He will make the arrangements.

Kowalski

The second note read:

Lange,

I'm so glad you could make it. I'm located in the army encampment on the other side of the monument. Come visit when you get a chance.

Pfeiffer

Lange considered which invitation he should accept first. The messenger's comment about showing his political demeanor was not lost. The SA was the chancellor's political army. A showing in that circle would give him prestige among those not so politically connected. An uncontrolled laugh finally cleared his throat as he thought of Kowalski as a group leader. He remembered how loathe Kowalski had been to take command of the platoon when Kluggmann was wounded and evacuated. And how, in the following year, Kowalski had earned the unteroffizier title and command of two platoons. They had lost track of one another when Lange had gone off to officers' school. Their paths had crossed during the evacuation of France. Kowalski had been leading an entire company, reduced by casualties and desertions to eighty men, back to Germany. Lange had absorbed Kowalski's company into his battalion. Jointly, they had led the men back to Germany for demobilization but not before they had paraded through the Berlin streets. He still remembered taking Kowalski's last salute as the two of them parted company at the Brandenburg Tor. Kowalski had trudged off to the east while Lange had gone north.

'And Pfeiffer? Still in the army and a general major.' Lange thought. He remembered that Pfeiffer had been reposted shortly after his lucky brush with death. There had been no fanfare of fare-well laced with promises of future help in getting out of the muck. Lange had woken one morning during a rest at the rear to find that the lieutenant was gone and a new company commander installed. Life had gone on amid the exploding shells. No-name soldiers had come and gone. Lange could see now that Pfeiffer had remained in the army and continued his rise.

Which meeting should he go to first?

His exploration of the camp took him from one end to the next and into the memorial's grounds guarded by men who could qualify as giants. Tall, lean armed with the new automatic pistols and dressed in black overcoats and helmets they were very impos-ing. They greeted Lange with a silent order arms and followed him with their eyes as he passed. The memorial was definitely a reverent place. Inside, people in various uniforms bustled about setting up chairs, viewing stands, and mournful decorations. He met many of his train mates during the walk. Over handshakes each made him promise to meet in the biergarten in the evening after a fitful nap and supper. Without hesitation, Lange agreed, somewhat to his dismay the words had leaped from his mouth before reason could quell them, to the rendezvous. Supper was a myriad of sausages, potatoes, and sweet wines. Many of the veterans laughingly shouted for hard tack but their demands were ignored. Then, as if they were still in the army, the diners arose from the tables to reconstitute themselves in the biergarten at the center of the encampment during the twilight hour. They had become compatriots even though few knew one another from the war. The train trip was their only claim to a mutual experience. But demeanors had changed. Those affiliated with Hitler's political party separated themselves from the others by sitting at one table apart from the not so politically minded veterans. Old soldiers could pass to the political table but party members did not sit at the old soldiers' table. Nevertheless, all of them sang the old drinking songs, jokes flowed freely, and tales of remembered comrades crossed between listeners. A few eyes grew teary but someone would save the moment by reminding everyone about the estaminets in France with their sour wine, exuberant prices, and less than virtuous women. Many remembered the same women and compared prices for those women's favors. The ones who got the cheapest prices were hailed as cheapskates. Soon, the group became exhausted from laughing and hoarse from singing-shouting. Conversations then turned to wives and children. Photographs were passed from hand to hand to be admired. As the number of beers drunk increased, Lange's group grew more sullen while the politically inspired members' groups became louder and the mentioning of influential names grew more numerous. Lange took note that second class Iron Crosses were in abundance among Hitler's group and many of the wearers made sure that the medals were prominently displayed with other colored ribbons. A few of the party also wore wound badges on lapels or uniform breast pockets but there was no evidence that the wound had disfigured the wearer. Lange began to wonder if these party members who represented the Great War veterans were real warriors or back area demigods who had received their medals from falling in ditches when some part of the line, forty kilometers away, was being shelled. The party members ignored questions from Lange's group regarding which regiments they had served in. They could only say that so and so had personally decorated them at some nameless place. SA herders closed the biergarten at ten reminding the revelers that the next day was a solemn occasion and a clear head was needed. A few of the old veterans tried to resist but the lights were turned off and the kegs of beer were taken away. There was no choice but to retire.

A bugle call woke the camp that was still bathed in darkness. Torch carrying SA troops ran among the tents announcing that Hindenburg's funeral train was arriving. Without washing or shaving, men hurriedly dressed and descended to the straight white path that led from the railroad to the monument. Youths arranged them into formations after the veterans had found friends to stand with. Vials of rosewater were passed through the ranks and soon the air smelled of stale beer and overly sweet flowers. Lange stood among the first ranks smoothing the wrinkles out of his uniform with a flattened hand.

"Hier kommt!" was shouted as a line of torches bordering the road stood out in the predawn grayness. Lange noted that it was the time to "stand to" in anticipation of an enemy attack. All were assembled and vigilant. The torch line grew closer. A company of soldiers led by an officer on a horse came into view and solemnly proceeded. Behind the marching men came a caisson drawn by six jet black horses. On the caisson was a huge coffin with an equally large imperial flag draped over it. The command was given. "Achtung!" Boot heels clicked and all conversation died away as the caisson rolled past. Automatically, everyone's eyes followed the movement until it was out of sight behind the walls of the monument. Many were reminded of the tales they had heard of the torch lit processions of the Teutonic Knights. But Lange found a more bizarre sight. There were no crippled veterans among the crowd. Everyone stood on their own two legs while both arms were held firmly against their trousers seams.

"Break ranks!" the voice commanded. "The funeral will begin at nine. Be back in your groups thirty minutes before."

The veterans wandered back to their tents to bathe and shave.

www.ingramcontent.com/pod-product-compliance
Lightning Source LLC
Chambersburg PA
CBHW071156050326
40689CB00011B/2130